LOVE CAN BE LONELY

Colette felt Ian's hand on her arm. She pulled away, hugging herself tighter. "Colette, please...talk to me," Ian said.

"Don't worry, I am not going to make another scene...now please stay on your side of the seat."

Colette closed her eyes. She felt the tears coming and she felt so sorry for herself, a desperate feeling that even Abby was growing away from her. She leaned her head against the window of the car. The window felt cold. She looked out and she could see the waning moon.

Never had she felt so lonely.

DOUBLE STANDARD

Elizabeth Levy

AN AVON FLARE BOOK

AVON BOOKS
A division of
The Hearst Corporation
1790 Broadway
New York, New York 10019

Copyright © 1984 by Elizabeth Levy
Published by arrangement with the author
Library of Congress Catalog Card Number: 84-91080
ISBN: 0-380-87379-6

First Flare Printing, July, 1984

FLARE TRADEMARK REG. U.S. PAT. OFF. AND IN
OTHER COUNTRIES, MARCA REGISTRADA, HECHO
EN U.S.A.

Printed in the U.S.A.

WFH 10 9 8 7 6 5 4 3 2 1

To Bonnie and Nan—
my double standards

DOUBLE STANDARD

Chapter One

Colette planted her feet near the edge of the small wooden platform and leaned her body closer to Abby's to pick up the harmony. She glanced down at the audience and knew it was a mistake. There he was again, just like he had been at the earlier show. The stranger. He watched, but when he caught Colette's eye, his ears turned a bright pink.

"You've got a groupie," whispered Abby as they played the instrumental break in the song. Colette pretended to kick her. Abby hopped back, grinning. She pointed her electric bass at Colette as if it were a weapon.

They ended the song. Colette rubbed her sweaty hands across the glitter headband she wore in her wavy hair. She bowed her head to acknowledge the applause. There he was—staring at her again!

Abby jumped up and down at the other end of the stage. She flashed Colette a signal, and they went into their last song, an old Beatles number. Colette caught a glimpse of her mother singing along, her hands clapping just a fraction behind the beat.

Colette moved across the stage so that she was right next to Abby. They made an odd couple. Colette was almost six inches taller than Abby. She was fair and snub-nosed to

Abby's petite dark looks. But they looked right together on stage.

Ever since she was very young, Colette had known she had a strong voice and perfect pitch. When she was little, her voice had embarrassed her. It was almost too powerful for a young girl. But then she had teamed up with Abby. They had begun harmonizing together as a joke, but soon they realized that their voices blended perfectly.

At first Colette was embarrassed to play in public. It made her self-conscious—as if she were being too noisy, calling too much attention to herself. "You're the only one I know who thinks that being the center of attention is a sin," teased Abby.

Colette remembered reading that Elvis Presley was so shy in high school that he would only play for his friends if they turned out the lights. He was just fifteen when he picked up his guitar, exactly their age.

Colette figured that if Elvis had had a friend like Abby, he would have been a happier man. Abby didn't seem to know the meaning of the word *shy*. She had talked Colette into playing before their friends, and soon they were getting paid for performing at parties. Now today, here they were at the school fair.

The Clarion Fall Fair was not a rinky-dink little event. Even the Boston newspapers gave the fair a full page. Clarion was Cambridge's oldest private school, almost as old as Harvard itself, and located just a few blocks from Harvard Square. Clarion prided itself on the fact that it was the first school in the nation to accept free blacks and Jews?

"But are they ready for a female, Jewish, rock-and-roll group?" Colette had joked to Abby.

"Is the world ready?" Abby asked. "There's only one way to find out."

As they neared the end of their last song, Colette and Abby got the audience clapping and singing with them. They fought to keep the audience's singing from throwing them off. Colette reached for a high note. She missed and felt rather than saw Abby's wince.

"Sorry," muttered Colette.

Abby paid no attention to her apology. Colette put the false note out of her mind as they hit the last chord. Abby reached across the stage for Colette's hand and held it up in the air as if Colette were a prizefighter who had won in the last round.

They took a final bow and jumped off the wooden platform. Colette unplugged her guitar and started to put it away.

"That was some high note you hit," said Abby.

"Yeah. Well, anything for art," said Colette.

"Honey, you were terrific." Colette's mother pushed up to the stage. "You were good, too, Abby. In fact, you were both terrific. I loved it."

"Thanks, Mom." Colette flinched at her mother's touch. Lately she realized that she was constantly being unfair to her mother. It was as if her mother just couldn't say or do anything right. Colette hated herself for feeling that way. It seemed like such a cliché of how a teenager should feel, but she couldn't stop herself. Abby told her to lighten up about it, that her mother was just the nervous type. Colette was scared that she had inherited her mother's nervous genes.

"Come on, Colette, we've got to clear the stage," said Abby. "They've got a bunch of clog dancers coming on in half an hour."

"I don't know why they don't schedule you last," said Colette's mother. "Nobody can concentrate after you two have been on. You're such a natural high."

"I don't know," said Abby. "I thought we reached a kind of unnatural high back there."

"What do you mean?" asked Colette's mother warily.

"I just meant Colette's missed note," said Abby. "Come on, Colette."

They started to pack up their equipment. For just a two-person band they had a lot. Abby had a portable electric piano as well as the bass. Colette had an electric guitar and a saxophone. Just then Ms. Anderson, Colette's favorite teacher, came up to the stage. She was dressed in black slacks pegged tightly at the ankle and a butter-soft purple suede jacket that bloused out at the hips.

"You girls were great," said Ms. Anderson. "I can't tell you how much I like to see girls doing rock and roll."

"It's so liberating to see girls 'rocking,'" echoed Colette's mother. "I just wish it were me up there on the stage instead of them."

"Well, then you should do it," said Ms. Anderson.

Colette giggled.

Her mother looked doubtful. "I suppose you're right."

"After all," said Ms. Anderson. "Colette had to inherit her talent from someone."

"I always thought she got it just because I named her Colette. I wanted her to have a name she could look up to."

Colette was named after her mother's favorite writer, a French woman who wrote about love. In her mother's study hung a photograph of the original Colette. There was humor in her eyes as if she knew a secret. It was an old photograph, taken in 1906. It showed a rather short woman with stocky thighs, standing with one breast bare. That breast both embarrassed and intrigued Colette. It was hard to think of someone that long ago posing half-nude.

Like her namesake, Colette had big breasts, but she could never imagine showing them in public. They embarrassed her. She thought they made her look fat, and she envied Abby for being flat-chested.

Colette had never had a nickname. She

often wondered what she would be like if she had a more common name. Once when she was about ten, she had decided that she wanted to be called 'Collie.' She thought it sounded nice and friendly. Her mother was horrified. "My God, you are named after a great woman, a woman never afraid to live life to the fullest. You can't throw that away and name yourself after a dog."

Occasionally Colette and Abby played a game in which they imagined they had different names. "I'd like to be either Erica or Ashley," said Colette. "My first choice would be Erica. No one can make a nickname out of it."

"I don't think you'd be a good Ashley," said Abby. "But you could be an Erica. Ericas are usually okay, if they're not snotty. But Ashleys are nosy. Now, for myself, I'd like to be called Tracey."

"Tracey," hooted Colette. "Traceys are little pink and blond girls who have a dozen Fair Isle sweaters in different shades of heather. Traceys never wear glitter. You'd make a lousy Tracey. How about Samantha? That's a pretty name."

"Samantha Klein? I don't think it goes. You're lucky. A name like 'Gordon' goes with anything. It doesn't sound so obviously Jewish."

With her light brown hair and small nose, most people didn't know that Colette was Jewish although she never tried to hide it. Yet Colette was aware that she had moments, particularly around Christmastime when all

of Cambridge looked like a movie set for
caroling, that she would like to be Christian.
And it made her extremely uneasy that she
could "pass." Abby, on the other hand, looked
Jewish and had a Jewish-sounding name,
but even she admitted that she had moments when she wished she didn't look *so*
Jewish.

Religion wasn't a subject that came up
often, but in the Waspy world of Cambridge
and of Clarion, it was a subject that always
seemed just beneath the surface.

Sometimes Colette felt guilty that she
could "pass" for being non-Jewish and Abby
couldn't. Abby told her that she was being
silly. There was nothing for her to feel guilty
about. In theory, there was no prejudice
against Jews in Cambridge, yet Cambridge
was a very Wasp town, particularly the private schools of Cambridge. Although no one
talked much about being Jewish, Colette and
Abby were always aware of which of their
friends were Jewish and which weren't. It
wasn't as if either of their families were
particularly religious. But Colette was always conscious of the fact that she *was* Jewish, even if she didn't look it.

"You're a little bananas on the subject, you
know," said Abby. "I'd love to have a name
like Colette Gordon. It's so much more unusual than Abby Klein. Maybe if I get famous I'll change my name."

"There's nothing wrong with Abby Klein."

"Nothing right with it, either," said Abby.
"It's sort of like my body, blah."

"Your body is not blah," argued Colette. "Stop putting yourself down."

Abby laughed. "Maybe I'll change my name to Colette, too. Then we can have a band called The Colettes."

"It sounds like something you take to make your breath smell sweet."

Actually, by the time she was thirteen, Colette decided, her name wasn't that bad. She'd even begun to read her namesake's books in the original French for school. The stories were often about young women and their affairs with older men. It was strange to think about teenagers, so many years ago, having sex.

While Colette and Abby finished packing up their equipment, several classmates gathered around to congratulate them. "Today the Clarion book fair, tomorrow we open for the Culture Club," said Abby.

Colette started to lug one of her amps over to her mother's car.

"Let me help you with that," said a voice at her shoulder.

Colette turned to face the boy who had been watching her. The stranger. He looked young, maybe fourteen, with a slightly round and soft look to his face. He wasn't chubby exactly, but he wasn't lean. He had straight, thick, light brown hair and hazel eyes. He gave Colette the impression that he could be easily hurt. Colette had often fantasized that someone lean, tall, and mysterious would see her play and want to meet her. But this boy didn't fit her fantasy. His ears stuck out a little and they were still a bright pink. Colette wondered if maybe they were permanently flushed.

"You were really good," he said.

"Thanks," said Colette. Colette knew that she didn't take compliments well. They embarrassed her. She sounded more curt and short-tempered than she felt. After all, it wasn't as if strange boys came up to her all the time and told her she was good. She smiled.

"I'm Ian Mitchell." He stuck out his hand. Colette almost laughed out loud. Nobody she knew shook hands. Colette took his hand and noticed that it was cool and dry. Her hand still felt sweaty from the performance. Their hands hung there in space. There was no electricity, no spark, yet Colette felt herself grow unaccountably warm. She pulled back her hand.

"Nice to meet you," she said. "I'm glad you liked the show."

"Where does this amp go?" he asked.

Colette pointed to her mother's blue Valiant. "Thanks for lugging it. I know it's heavy."

"That's okay. I'm stronger than I look."

Colette felt embarrassed for him. She felt it was the kind of dumb remark she might make. "Me, too," she said.

The boy smiled at her again. "Well, you already look pretty strong. I mean . . . your arms are strong from playing the guitar, I guess."

Colette looked down at her well-muscled

arms. She did have more upper body strength than most girls, and he was right, it did come from playing the guitar. Most people didn't realize that being a rock musician was a very physical job.

"Where are you from?" Colette asked. She knew she had never seen him before.

"Uhh . . . I'm a junior at Andover."

Andover was a boarding school several miles north of Boston. Colette didn't know anyone who went there, but her assumption was that most of the students were snobs. Either that or they were kids who hated their homes and had parents who wanted to get rid of them.

Colette wondered if Ian was a snob. She was surprised that he was a junior. That would make him older than she was. He must be at least sixteen.

"What grade are you in?" Ian asked.

"I'm a sophomore." Colette looked across the fairgrounds. Abby was walking away from their friends and coming toward them.

"Hi," said Abby as she reached them. Her long dark hair was matted to her head with sweat. She, too, really worked out during a performance. "How did you like the show?"

"Do you two know each other?" Colette asked.

Ian's ears turned pink again. Colette wished that they wouldn't do that so easily.

"No, we don't know each other. But I saw you looking at us when we were performing. I'm Abby Klein," said Abby. She stuck out her hand to Ian. Now Colette felt silly for having thought badly of Ian for shaking hands. She wished she could talk to this boy as easily as Abby could.

"Ian Mitchell. I liked your act."

"Yeah, we could see you did," said Abby. She gave a secret little grin to Colette.

"What are you doing at Clarion's fair?" Abby asked him.

"I came in with a group of guys. They split for the Square. I stayed. I caught your first act, and somebody told me you were going on again. You two are terrific."

"Thanks. But I don't think you noticed me too much. I saw you staring at Colette."

Colette groaned to herself.

"No, you were both terrific," said Ian quickly. "You play real tight. Like you've been playing together for a long time."

"We've been playing together since we were about ten."

Colette saw her mother coming toward them. She felt nervous about introducing her to this boy. "Look, excuse us," she said. "We've got to join some friends. I'm glad you liked the show."

Colette held on to Abby's forearm and moved her away. She made a point of not looking back at Ian. "Gee, you're real nice to the fans," said Abby.

"Fan," corrected Colette. "He was sort of a nerd, don't you think?" Colette didn't want to admit that she had liked Ian.

"He wasn't. He was sweet."

"His ears stick out and they turn pink."

"I think that's cute," argued Abby.

"It's cute on a pink elephant." Colette sighed. She wished they were back up on the stage. Up on stage was one of the few places she could stop thinking and just *be*. Almost everywhere else, she heard a voice in her head, constantly criticizing herself, thinking twice, as if she were watching herself in a movie, and the movie wasn't very good. Coming down from a performance always made her feel strange, as if she had too much energy, too much movement in her legs, just too much of everything. She found it hard to concentrate, particularly on any one person.

Perhaps she had been too abrupt with Ian. After all, he had sought her out. He had made her feel special, even if he was just ordinary-looking. She wished now that she hadn't brushed him off. She looked around for him, but he was gone.

"What's wrong?" Abby asked.

"Nothing, just the blues, I guess. It's silly to get depressed at a school fair."

"Who knows . . . maybe it's silly *not* to get depressed at a school fair."

Colette laughed, somehow feeling better. Abby could always make her laugh, always did. Their first meeting was now a legend. When they were infants, they were in the same playgroup. In a room full of other babies, Abby and Colette had crawled straight to each other and begun to giggle. They had been giggling together ever since.

Chapter Two

It was the week after the Clarion Fair. Colette was alone in the house. Her father and mother were at a party. Colette liked having the house to herself. They lived in a small house, by Cambridge standards. A beautiful blue fir tree stood outside, like a perfect Christmas tree, but the tree blocked most of the possible southern light. In order to save money, Colette's parents kept the house at sixty-two degrees during the winter. A woodburning stove stood in the kitchen, and the living room had a fireplace, but the house was almost always cool. Even tonight when it was just mid-October, the house was quite cold. But Colette liked it. The cool air made her feel alive.

She was working on an English assignment and wishing she could just forget about it and practice the guitar. She was sweating over her essay. Writing never came easy to her. She was in the middle of a thought when the phone rang.

"Help, I'm a prisoner inside a boob tube," whispered a voice.

"Abb?" Colette knew that Abby was babysitting for neighbors.

"It's *moi.* I'm watching a Godzilla movie on TV. But I've seen it before, so I thought I'd give you a call."

"Did you get the kids asleep okay?"

"Yeah, these kids are no problem. What are you doing?"

"That English essay. I hate it. I hate nineteenth-century poetry. It sucks."

"Better not let my mom hear you," said Abby. Abby's mother was an English teacher at a public high school in the suburbs.

"Did you do the assignment?" Colette asked.

"Yeah, I finished it. That's why I'm watching Godzilla. I wonder if I'll ever get to write about Godzilla."

"I haven't finished the stupid assignment," said Colette. "Do you think it'll be all right if I don't do it? I really want to practice that new song we were trying out. Don't you think it'd be all right? I could say I did it and it got lost."

Abby hesitated. Colette frequently got in trouble for getting her assignments in late and for the fact that she handed them in so messy. "I think maybe you should do it and get it over with," warned Abby.

Colette swore. "Well, maybe I'll find time to do it. Don't make me feel guilty about not doing the assignment. I was hoping you would tell me it was all right."

Over the years Colette and Abby had gotten into the habit of telling each other, "It's all right if I . . ."

"It's all right if I don't finish the assignment."

"It's all right if I told a white lie."

"It's all right if I hate my little sister."

"Look," said Abby. "I can't stay on the phone too long. These people always call to check on how I'm doing. Do the assignment. It's not that bad."

"Okay, I'll talk to you later." Colette hung up, feeling vaguely dissatisfied. She was scared about what would happen if she and Abby stopped saying "It's all right" to each other.

The phone rang again. Colette figured it was Abby. Abby had an uncanny knack for realizing when Colette was feeling hurt. She just knew it was Abby calling back because that last phone call had been ever-so-slightly creepy. Abby would call back and make everything all right again.

Colette reached for the receiver. Her hand hovered above it, and she could feel the vibrations.

"Abbadaba," whispered Colette, using her old nickname for Abby.

"Excuse me," said a male voice. He sounded as if he had a cold. Colette was so flustered that she hung up the phone. Seconds later the phone rang again. Colette let it ring nearly six times before she answered it.

"Hello," she said tentatively into the phone.

"Is this the Gordon residence?" asked the voice.

"Who do you want to speak to?" Colette

asked. Her father had taught her to answer a question with a question on the telephone. "You don't 'owe' anyone information," he told her. "Sometimes burglars want to find out if you're alone. Make the person calling tell you what they want."

"I'd like to speak to Colette Gordon," said the voice. Colette stared at the receiver. She didn't recognize the voice.

"Is this Colette?" he asked. He sounded as if he was trying to make his voice lower.

"Who is this?" Colette asked.

"It's Ian Mitchell." His voice was now pitched so low that Colette had trouble hearing it.

At the sound of his name, Colette drew her feet underneath her like a contented cat. "Oh, sure . . . hi," she said.

A vision of pink ears floated in front of Colette's eyes. Pink ears—and a vague warm feeling that here was someone who actually thought she was special. Colette had felt bad that he hadn't asked for her telephone number, and she hadn't expected ever to hear from him. "How did you get my number?" she asked.

"I always get *A*'s for research. Actually, it wasn't hard. You're well-known around Clarion."

"I should be. I've gone there since kindergarten. But who do you know at Clarion?"

"I have connections," he said mysteriously. "It must be strange to be at the same school

all your life. You've known the same kids
forever."

Colette wondered if he was putting her
down, putting down the fact that she had
been in the same place all her life.

"Where are you from?" she asked.

"New York. But don't get the wrong idea.
My parents aren't divorced. They aren't trying to get rid of me by sending me to boarding school. I was the one who wanted to
go."

"Hey, you don't have to get so defensive
with me," Colette protested.

"I'm sorry. But kids who go to day schools
always think that if you go to boarding school
you're either a snob, or your parents want to
get rid of you."

Colette remained silent for a second. That
was exactly what she had first thought of
him. This was a strange conversation to be
happening between two people who didn't
even know each other. Colette rearranged
her legs underneath her. She glanced out the
window. She could see leaves falling in the
cold autumn rain. The street looked slick in
the light of the streetlamp that shone into
her bedroom window. Colette could remember as a little girl waking up early and
waiting for the streetlamp to go off so that
the day would start.

"I wanted to know if I could see you,"
Ian said. His voice cracked on the word
see.

Colette wondered if his ears had turned

pink again. "You mean, you want to hear Abby and me sing again?" she teased.

"Uh . . . no. I mean, I'd like to hear you sing again, I really would, but I was thinking about just a date."

"A date?" Colette heard her own voice crack. She wondered what Ian would think if he ever found out that even though she was fifteen and a half, she still hadn't gone out on an official date. Neither had Abby.

Everyone at Clarion knew each other so well that almost no one dated. Abby joked about it. "We're all such good friends that it's like we have a pact," complained Abby. "The Moral Majority has nothing on us. We're going to be the first class to graduate as virgins."

Abby was exaggerating, but she was partly right. Somehow no one in their particular group seemed to have an active sex life. They hung out together, boys and girls, but they didn't date. Every once in a while, two would pair off together, but so far it hadn't happened to either Colette or Abby. They had begun to joke that they were going to have to start some rumors soon, or their parents would be convinced they were gay.

"A date?" Colette echoed.

"What's the matter, is it a dirty word?"

"Depends what you had in mind." Colette couldn't believe she had said that. Why was she saying such stupid, teasing things?

"How about Friday night?" Ian had the decency to ignore her crack. "I noticed the

Beatles movie, *A Hard Day's Night* is playing in the Square," he said. "I thought maybe you'd like to see it."

Colette wished that he had suggested anything else. "Uhh . . . Abby and I were going to see that together. You see, we play a lot of Beatles music, and I promised I'd go see it with her." Colette felt foolish. She felt like she was blabbering. Yet she had promised Abby, and it wouldn't feel right to go to the movie without her.

"I could bring in a friend for Abby. We could double-date."

"Double-date?" Colette giggled. "It sounds like something from a fifties movie." She winced. She was talking like a complete idiot. "That would be terrific. See, Abby and I don't just perform together, we're best friends, and it would be neat if we could go together." Now she sounded like a blabbering fool. "I'll call Abby and see if she'll double-date."

"Okay, thanks. I'll call you tomorrow night and we can make plans." Ian got off the phone quickly. Colette wondered if he regretted his phone call. She wished now that she had the number where Abby was baby-sitting.

The next morning, Colette picked Abby up at her house on the way to school. Abby walked with her head down, kicking at the dead leaves.

"How was your baby-sitting job?" Colette asked.

"Okay." Abby lifted her head. "I'm sorry I lectured you about that homework assignment. I felt awful that I didn't say, 'It's all right.' Then I tried to call you back, but the phone was busy. I was worried that maybe you were mad and had taken it off the hook."

"I finally did the homework assignment, the poetry one." Colette felt relieved that Abby had tried to call her back. And she was glad that she could tell Abby that she had done the homework assignment.

"Great," said Abby. "Now you don't have to worry about telling a lie."

"So," said Colette, feeling good and eager to tell Abby about Ian's phone call. "How would you like a date this weekend?"

Abby threw her arms around Colette. "Oh, God, thank heaven. You've finally asked me out. Oh, Colette, if you only knew how I've longed for this moment."

"Laugh all you want. But I'm serious. We are finally going to embark on the adventure of teenage romance. It's about time."

"But a date," simpered Abby. "A real date. Will you pay for my movie?"

"Cut it out. That kid from Andover called me, remember, the one with the pink ears? He asked me out on Friday night, to go see *A Hard Day's Night*. If he likes the Beatles, he can't be all bad. I said that I had plans to see that movie with you, and he offered to bring a friend for you."

"Pour moi!" exclaimed Abby in her best Miss Piggy voice.

"Yeah. Well, I don't know who he'll bring,

but it could be someone fantastic. Unless all guys at Andover have pink ears."

"Stop going on about his pink ears. He was nice."

"Okay, he's nice," Colette admitted, wishing that she hadn't almost choked on the word *nice*. "Anyhow, will you come? He's calling me back tonight to find out if it's okay."

"Sure, who am I to turn down a blind date? I haven't yet had a seeing one! You know, maybe this is just what we need."

"What do you mean, what we need?" asked Colette.

"I mean," explained Abby, "that it's time we did something to earn our reputation. Everyone thinks you and I are wild just because we play rock. Only at Clarion could two virgins get to be known as the wild and crazy ones. We get the reputation and we don't do anything. Besides, I wonder which of us is supposed to be wild and which one crazy?"

"Which do you want to be?" Colette asked.

Abby considered the question. "I get to pick?"

Colette made an elaborate bowing motion. "Sure, you get first choice. I'll take the one left over."

"Wild or crazy. It's a big decision. Can I choose later?" Abby asked. "You wouldn't want me to just pick the first thing that came into my mind."

"No, no, of course not," said Colette. "Besides, maybe your date will help you choose!"

Chapter Three

On Friday night, Abby went over to Colette's house to wait for Ian and his friend to pick them up. They holed up in Colette's room, putting final touches on their makeup. Abby wasn't very good at it. Her hand shook as she put on her eyeliner.

"Will you finish my makeup for me?" Abby asked. She tilted her face up to Colette. Colette patted on a bit of the glitter shadow they had bought together at Harvard Square. It made Abby's eyes sparkle.

Abby looked critically at herself in the mirror. She was dressed in a bright red sweat-shirt minidress. The tight-knit ribs of the dress clung, emphasizing her small waist and small breasts. Colette wished she didn't have such large breasts, so that she could wear something like that.

Colette was dressed in brand new beige culottes and a purple, pleated, gauzy blouse with a thin stripe of silvery glitter through it. In the right light, you could see the outline of her bra.

Abby frowned at herself in the mirror. "Do you think I look cheap?" she asked.

"Are you kidding? You look fantastic. I mean it, you look just beautiful. You don't look cheap. You look like a class act." Colette studied herself in the mirror. "Do I look frumpy?"

Abby looked at her critically. "The blouse is terrific."

"The pants?"

Abby shrugged. "They look like they belong on your mother. You look better in jeans."

Colette tugged at the wide pants of the culottes. They did look awfully preppy. She didn't want to hurt her mother by not wearing them, but lately, whenever she shopped with her mother, they ended up buying something that she didn't like once she got it home.

"They look good," said Abby. "They just don't look . . ." She searched for the right word.

"Awesome?"

Abby giggled. "You know that wasn't the word I was searching for. They look fine, honest."

Quickly, Colette went into her closet and pulled out her jeans. Her closet was a mess, as usual. Sometimes she thought the floor of it had a magnet that attracted her clothes. Abby, although few people besides Colette knew it, had a closet that was a marvel of neatness, a fact that never ceased to amaze Colette. Abby's sweaters were folded and lined up precisely in the colors of the rainbow. Her closet always looked as if it were about to be featured in *Seventeen*. Abby didn't like to be teased about the fact that she was so neat. She thought she was a freak of nature, a neat teenager. Colette assured her that nobody who knew her would ever think she was uptight. Her closet was just one of the seven wonders of the world.

Colette slipped out of her culottes and struggled into her jeans. They were so tight that she had to lie down on the bed to zip them up. She stood up and looked at herself in the full-length mirror.

The jeans seemed to emphasize the prettiness of the blouse. It had dozens of pleats in it. Colette tugged at the top, making the pleats expand, then released them, allowing them to contract. She pulled them out again, pushed them in again. "It's like an accordion."

"Are you going to let Ian play it?" Abby asked.

Colette threw a pillow at her. She straddled the chair of her vanity table and dabbed glitter makeup on her eyelids. She liked the way she looked now that she had the culottes off—less preppy, more sexy.

"Do you think I look too dressed up?" Abby asked.

Colette shook her head. "No, you look just right."

"Do you know the name of my date?"

"No. Watch, he'll be gorgeous." Colette tried to make her voice sound light, to make it seem as if she were joking, but in truth she was more than a little jealous that Abby was getting a chance with a perfect stranger. *Perfect* was the operable word. A stranger might just, against all possible odds, turn out to be perfect, while she, Colette, would be with Ian. It wasn't that she didn't like Ian. She did. Talking with him on the phone had made her feel good. Yet somehow she didn't think that Ian was going to be the great romance of her life.

Colette looked out the window, hoping she would be able to catch a glimpse of Ian and his friend before they arrived. Her father was at a meeting, but her mother was down in the basement, working in her darkroom. Colette wanted to be sure that *she* and not her mother let the boys in.

Finally the door bell rang. "I'll get it," screamed Colette. Abby came clomping down the stairs. Her clogs sounded like a machine gun on the bare wooden floor.

Colette opened the door. Ian was dressed all in beige. He wore a beige corduroy jacket over a beige sweater. His beige down jacket hung open. Beige, beige, beige, thought Colette. Then he smiled at her.

Colette thought how much his smile changed his face. When he wasn't smiling he looked a little too much like a bookworm, a person who took everything too seriously. But he had an impish smile, a little bit like the smile of her namesake, the French writer. Colette wondered whether she'd ever tell him that he had a smile that made him look like he was keeping a secret.

Colette smiled back. The boy standing next to Ian grinned at them. "So you're the god-

dess who's got Mitchell hot and bothered."
Colette felt herself blush. She looked up into
a pair of blue eyes, the blue all the more
surprising because the boy was so dark.
He looked as if he hadn't lost an iota
of his summer tan. He had thick black hair
that he wore somewhat long, with flopping
bangs on his forehead. He was thin, dressed
in a bluish-gray tweed sports jacket and
jeans.

"I'm Colette Gordon, Ian's date." She stuck
out her hand to shake his, remembering too
late that she had ridiculed Ian for shaking
hands.

"Abernathy, Jim Abernathy."

"Come on in," said Colette. Abby stood
with one foot on the stairs, looking surprisingly shy. "Abby, this is Jim Abernathy. You
met Ian at the fair."

Jim dwarfed Abby. He must have been
nearly six feet tall. "Hi, Abby. Call me
Abernathy. Everybody does. Ian didn't tell
me you were so cute." He reached out and
tousled Abby's long hair as if she were a
poodle that he found just adorable. Then he
turned and looked at Colette.

"That's a beautiful blouse."

"Thank you." Colette struggled to keep her
voice from trembling.

"Very sexy," said Abernathy. "But you
shouldn't wear a bra with it. It ruins the
look."

Colette did a double take. None of the
magazines ever told you what to say to a boy

who tells you that you shouldn't wear a bra, especially if that boy was incredibly sexy and your best friend's date. He stood there smiling at her so casually, as if he hadn't just flustered her completely.

"I said, you shouldn't wear a bra with that blouse. The pleats would look beautiful if your breasts were free underneath."

Colette felt herself blush. "Look, Jim . . ." She wasn't exactly sure how she was going to end that sentence. "Look, Jim," sounded like a feeble beginning.

"Call me Abernathy—it's so much more informal."

Abby let out a high-pitched giggle.

"Don't mind him," said Ian. "He practices those lines in front of the mirror every night."

Abernathy flashed Ian a dirty look. Ian shrugged it off.

"I'm sorry," said Ian to Colette.

"You shouldn't have to apologize for your friend." Colette glanced again at Abernathy.

Abernathy had turned back to Abby. He leaned against the doorway to the living room, his left arm supporting his weight. Abby was looking up at him. They looked like a stereotype of teenagers in love.

"You have a nice home," said Ian. "It's unusual." He was looking at the many black-and-white photographs hanging on the hallway walls.

"My mom's an amateur photographer. She took most of these pictures."

"She's good." Ian studied the pictures closely.

Colette nodded. She thought her mother's pictures were beautiful. Her mother specialized in portraits of her family. Colette always thought she looked prettier in those photographs than she did in real life.

Ian continued to examine the pictures on the wall, pictures of Colette since she was a baby. She felt exposed, as if he were finding out too much about her too fast. "Shouldn't we be leaving?" she asked anxiously. "I mean, if you guys wanted to get to the movie."

Ian looked at his watch, a black plastic watch with a calculator and a stopwatch on it. Colette felt annoyed at him for having a calculator on his watch, and then annoyed at herself for being so picky.

"The movie doesn't start for half an hour. Abernathy and I picked up tickets on our way here. We didn't want to have to worry about it being sold out. We've got plenty of time."

Just then, Colette heard her mother's footsteps coming up from the basement. Her mother had promised Colette that she wouldn't make a big deal out of meeting her date. "I remember how embarrassed I used to be when your grandmother used to beam at my dates," she had said. "I'll just be doing some catch-up work in the basement darkroom. I'll pay you no mind."

Now she walked into the living room, carrying a short piece of clothesline from which hung several fresh, wet photographs. Colette hoped that none of them were of her and Abby performing at the Clarion Fair. Even though her mother had taken some terrific shots of them onstage, Colette didn't want Ian and Abernathy to see them right now. Abernathy gave her mother a polite nod as if they already knew each other.

"Mom, I'd like you to meet Ian Mitchell and Jim Abernathy." Ian stuck out his hand and then quickly drew it back again as he realized that Colette's mother didn't have a free hand.

"How do you do, boys? Don't mind me. I'm just passing through."

"I was admiring your photographs," said Ian. "You're really good."

"Thanks. I've had the good luck to have a photogenic daughter." She glanced at Colette, taking in the fact that she was not wearing the culottes they had bought together. "You've changed," she said.

"Abby felt the jeans looked better with my blouse." Colette spoke quickly and knew she sounded defensive.

Ian seemed to sense her unease. "We'd better be going. It was nice to meet you, Mrs. Gordon. Does Colette have a curfew?"

Colette's mother guffawed. "I'm sorry," she said, trying to choke back a laugh. "You brought back such memories. First of all, Colette's friends call me Maggie, and I'd like you to do that, too. Second of all, curfews seem so old-fashioned. We trust Colette's judgment."

Colette wondered how her parents had decided that they could trust her judgment when she hadn't ever been on a date before. Her mother made her sound like a goody-two-shoes. She told herself to stop being so hard on her mother. Her mother sounded fine, and Ian had liked her photographs. Colette just wished that they were out of the house.

"Good night, honey. Have a good time."

Colette gave her mother a hug. "You're beaming," she warned. But she gave her mother an extra tight squeeze and kissed her on the cheek.

"Good night, Maggie," said Abby. She and Abernathy walked out the door. Colette grabbed her jacket. Ian took its sleeve and tried to hold it for her. They had an awkward tussle in the foyer while Colette struggled to get her arm in the sleeve. The jacket seemed to have grown tentacles, as if it had a life of its own.

"I'm sorry," said Ian as he tugged at her jacket, wrapping Colette's arm behind her back. Finally, between the two of them, they got her arms into the sleeves and the jacket on her back. Colette felt as if together they had won some kind of a victory.

"Don't apologize. It was my fault. I guess I'm not used to anybody holding my jacket for me."

"Okay, I apologize for apologizing."

Colette glanced over at him to see if he was teasing. He looked at her and smiled a sort of half-mocking smile as if they had been sharing jokes together for a long time. Colette found herself laughing. Already she'd come to think of it as his impish smile. "Okay, your apology that was not needed is accepted."

"Good. Do you ever do that? Say you're sorry just to sort of fill in conversation? It makes you feel so stupid."

"Yeah, I do that a lot," admitted Colette. "Like sometimes at school someone might bump into me, I'll apologize, and the person looks at me as if I'm nuts. Then I find myself apologizing for apologizing."

"Like I just did," said Ian. "Well, at least we have that in common." He laughed again, but it wasn't a nervous laugh.

They walked to the Square, talking about the Beatles. Ian's favorite Beatle was Ringo. Colette decided she could understand that. Ringo had a sweetness to him that reminded her of Ian.

Up ahead, Abby and Abernathy walked along. She was looking up at him with a peculiar constant tossing of her head that looked phony to Colette.

"Is Abernathy a good friend of yours?" Colette asked.

"Sort of," said Ian. "He's got a great sense of humor. And he's got a car. He just turned seventeen."

"Did you guys drive in?" Colette asked. She felt excited. They had a car. None of the boys she and Abby knew drove yet. Abernathy having a car meant that they could go any-where if they wanted.

She was disappointed when Ian said, "No, we took the train. It's really easy for me to get into Cambridge." It seemed like Ian was trying to let her know that he could see her again if everything worked out.

"Don't you have curfews at Andover? Can you just go out whenever you want?"

"No, but on weekends we're pretty free. We just sign out. Abernathy's family has a house in Manchester, Massachusetts, not New Hampshire. Do you know where that is? It's a little town just north of here. It's right on the ocean."

Colette knew of it. One of the most popular girls at Clarion had a summer home there. But it was a girl with whom Colette had never felt comfortable. And she had never been invited to her big pajama parties by the shore.

Manchester was one of New England's perfect little resort towns. A few years back, the kids in Manchester had caused a scandal when they had T-shirts made up saying they belonged to NNJA. The Boston newspapers found out that NNJA meant "No Niggers or Jews Allowed."

"Yeah, I've heard of it," said Colette. "I remember reading about a nice little club the kids up there had. Was Abernathy a charter member?"

"Look, that was a bunch of public-school kids," said Ian, sounding annoyed that Colette would bring up something that unpleasant.

Colette felt as if she had transgressed, crossed a line that she shouldn't have. She looked ahead at Abernathy's perfect-fitting

sports jacket. She suspected that Abernathy
and Ian both came from a world where
"Jews" were thought to be too loud, too
pushy. She hadn't liked Ian's snobbish tone
when he said "a bunch of public-school kids,"
as if private-school kids couldn't be just as
secretly anti-Semitic. Both boys acted as if
money and the things that came with it were
to be taken for granted but never talked
about. It made Colette feel uneasy. They
seemed so Waspy.

"Well, Abby and I would be public-school
kids if we both didn't get scholarships to
Clarion," Colette snapped.

"What does that have to do with anything?" asked Ian.

The nice warm feelings and Ian's impish
grin were gone. He walked stiffly, making
Colette feel as if he didn't want to be with
her. And it had happened so quickly. Colette
wished she could say something that would
make everything feel comfortable again. But
she shouldn't have to apologize. Ian was the
one who was the snob.

Abby and Abernathy were waiting for
them at the corner, ready to cross the Cambridge Common, a park where cows once
had grazed in Colonial times, and where the
rebel army had fought the British. Now the
Common was full of joggers, soccer play-
ers, kids smoking joints, and mothers with
babies.

It must have been clear from the expres-
sions on Colette's and Ian's faces that some-

thing was wrong. "What's this?" asked Abernathy. "A lover's quarrel on the first date? How quaint."

"Stuff it, Abernathy," snapped Ian.

Abernathy laughed at him. "Touchy, touchy. Too bad Mitchell couldn't fall for someone like Abby." He smiled down at Abby. "You wouldn't give a fellow a hard time, would you? Not like your friend."

Abby gave Colette a confused look. "What's going on?" she asked in a worried voice.

"Nothing . . . forget it," said Colette. She glanced sideways at Ian. "Look," she whispered. "I'm sorry. I didn't mean to bring that crap up."

"It wasn't crap," said Ian.

Colette shook her head.

"No . . . it's me who should say, 'I'm sorry'. I don't even know what happened," said Ian. "I'm not even sure what we were fighting about."

"Neither am I," said Colette. But she was lying. Inside she did know what they had fought about. She and Ian came from different worlds. She could fake fitting into his world, but it made her nervous.

"Well, speaking of forgetting our troubles," said Abernathy, "I've got something here that will help."

"Oh," asked Abby warily. "What's that?"

Abernathy took out a joint. He waved it under Colette's nose. "You wouldn't want to go see *A Hard Day's Night* without this, would you? The music will sound much better. Although personally I've always thought the Beatles are overrated. However, I know that's heresy with Mitchell."

Colette tried not to stare at the joint. It was not as if she'd never seen one before, of course, but in seventh grade, she and Abby had made a pact not to smoke or use dope. So far they had stuck to it. Actually, it hadn't been hard. Most of the kids they hung out with didn't use dope. Colette wondered what Abby would do. She wondered what *she* would do.

Abernathy lit the joint and took a deep drag, sucking the smoke into his lungs. He handed it to Abby. She held it awkwardly. "Uh, I don't usually do this," she said. "In fact, uhh . . ."

Colette moved closer to Abby. "Maybe we should try it just this once," she whispered. She didn't want Ian to think they were so unsophisticated that they wouldn't even take a puff of a joint.

Abby giggled as she held the joint awkwardly between her thumb and forefinger. "Come on, little one, you're letting expensive stuff go to waste. It won't bite you," said Abernathy.

Abby handed the joint to Colette without taking a puff. Abernathy gave her an amused look. Colette held the joint in her hand, feeling like they were playing Hot Potato. She couldn't decide what to do. Was she going to go through her whole life without ever trying anything? She was sure that one puff wouldn't make her a drug addict. It was silly to call yourself a musician and never once try marijuana.

"Well, I guess there's a first time for everything," said Colette. The problem was that Colette had never inhaled anything, cigarette or marijuana. She took a puff and opened her mouth to say something to Abby. The smoke came pouring back out, none of it getting into her lungs. Colette started to choke. She passed the joint to Ian, who looked at her ironically. "I think I need practice," said Colette.

Ian shook his head. "Sorry—but I don't use the stuff. I get high on the Beatles anyhow."

I'm an idiot, Colette thought to herself. She had taken a puff to try to impress Ian, and he probably would have liked her better if she hadn't even tried.

Abernathy held the joint out to Abby. Abby shook her head.

"I thought you girls were such cool musicians. Ian said you both had fantastic voices."

"You don't have to be into dope to play music," said Colette. How come Ian could refuse the joint and sound just fine, while she sounded like a Drug Council TV ad?

Abernathy gave Colette a slow stare. "Well, I guess you and I will have to finish this together." He took another deep drag. "Unless . . . Abby, come on. Even Colette tried it. Won't you take a little puff just to please me?"

Colette couldn't stand his needling, coaxing voice. "Why does she have to do it to please you?" she asked.

"I can please myself," said Abby. "For God's sake, I thought it was supposed to make you happy. We sound like a debating society."

Ian laughed appreciatively. "Put it away, Abernathy. We don't need it to enjoy the movie."

"Tell me, Abby, do you think you have room for a very clean Ian Mitchell in your little group?"

"Why are you asking me?" said Abby. "Ian is Colette's date."

Abernathy put his arm around Colette, so that now he stood with a girl on each arm. Ian stood to the side, the outsider. Colette felt the strength in Abernathy's arm as he held her. Colette slipped out from under his arm and went and stood next to Ian. Ian put his arm around her waist. His touch was light compared to Abernathy's.

"Let's go," said Ian. "We don't want to be late for the movie."

Abernathy glanced backward at Colette. Was he challenging her? He seemed to be telling her that he knew he could take her from Ian by just a mere snap of his fingers. Strangely, although Colette had gone into the date with no feeling of loyalty to Ian, Abernathy made her feel protective of him. She wanted to prove Abernathy wrong.

"I'm sorry," said Ian, breaking into her thoughts.

"Not again," said Colette. "What are you sorry about?"

"I'm sorry Abernathy brought out that

joint. I could tell it made you and Abby uncomfortable, even though you tried it."

"Ian Mitchell, I'm going to make a deal with you. You stop saying 'I'm sorry' all the time, and I'll . . ." Colette paused. She couldn't think of what to use as her part of the deal.

"You'll kiss me good night," Ian said quickly.

Colette laughed. "You call that a deal?"

"A good one," said Ian.

Chapter Four

Once they got inside the theater, Colette lost herself in the utter joy of the movie. She noticed that Paul McCartney had a round, soft face, not unlike Ian's. And she decided that she liked Ringo better than she had ever liked him before. She loved the scene where he wandered alone through the streets of London with his camera, looking like a forlorn waif.

She watched the pictures of the Beatles fans. It seemed strange to think that they were no older than she was now. They looked so different, the girls in their bouffant hairdos and miniskirts. Even though she and Abby wore miniskirts, the miniskirts from the 1960s somehow looked different.

Ian didn't touch her in the movie, and Colette had mixed feelings about that. She would have liked to hold his hand when the Beatles sang "I Want to Hold your Hand," even if that was corny, but she didn't have the nerve to reach out for Ian's hand. Ian kept them in his lap. Every once in a while Colette stole a glance at him, but he never seemed to be looking at her.

Abernathy sat on the other side of her. He kept up a running commentary on the movie, designed to show how knowledgeable he was.

"Look at that blonde," he said during one scene. "That's the girl who married George Harrison. They met in the movie.

"Did you get that when Lennon put the Coke bottle up his nose? A lot of people miss it.

"They were going to call the movie 'Beatle-mania' until after they finished filming it. Ringo kept using the phrase 'A Hard Day's Night,' and Paul and John decided to write a song about it. Then it got to be the name of the movie."

Colette knew some of the things he was telling her, and she found his superior whisper a turnoff. He would aim his remarks first at Abby, but he always whispered in a voice loud enough so that Colette could hear.

Then he would turn to Colette and whisper the same things, but this time he would put his mouth practically right on her ear and whisper the words in a breathy voice.

Colette wanted to tell him to shut up, or at least to keep his remarks to Abby, but she didn't have the nerve. Abernathy laughed loudly at all the Beatles' antics, but his voice sounded false, like someone who was trying to pretend he was high.

When the movie ended, Ian clapped whole-heartedly.

"He thinks it's live and they can hear him," whispered Abernathy into Colette's ear. His tongue actually grazed her earlobe.

Colette twisted away from him. As the credits rolled, she watched the stills of the

Beatles flash across the screen. Then the lights went on.

"That was wonderful," she said to Ian. "I loved it." She deliberately kept her back to Abernathy.

"Me, too. I could stay and see it right through again."

Abernathy groaned. "Spare me." He had his arm around Abby. "I've got better plans for the rest of the evening."

"I was only kidding," said Ian. Colette wished that he didn't sound so defensive.

They left the theater. Out on the sidewalk, Colette started to sing one of the Beatles songs. At first she sang softly, but then the pure joy from the movie got to her, and she sang full out. Ian joined her. Abby broke in, and surprisingly, the three of them didn't sound bad together. They did a little dance on the sidewalk, imitating Ringo's shadow-boxing motion. Colette and Ian threw fake punches at each other, sparring and laughing. Ian did a sort of hop and fake jump, just like Ringo.

Abby stopped and fell into step with Abernathy. Her face was flushed. Colette and Ian kept dancing on the sidewalk. "You're making a spectacle of yourselves," Abernathy said.

"What happens when you get two monocles together?" Ian asked.

"I don't know," said Abby.

"They make spectacles of themselves."

Everyone laughed except Abernathy.

They decided to go to Bailey's for ice cream. Colette and Abby insisted on paying.

"You guys paid for the movie. Fair is fair," said Colette.

"Forget it," said Ian, taking out his wallet. "I was the one to ask you out. You can take me out the next time."

"How do you know there will be a next time?" said Abernathy. "Maybe we should take advantage of it now."

"This isn't up for discussion," said Abby. "We're paying. How do you think we spend all that money we make performing at parties? Well, it's not so much. It barely pays for new music and stuff, but this is our treat!"

"Very cute," said Abernathy. He put his hand over Ian's and helped Ian put his wallet away. While they were taking their sundaes to the tables in the back, Abby fell in step next to Colette. "Come to the bathroom with me," she whispered. "I've got to talk to you."

Colette nodded. She felt the need to talk to Abby, too. All night, their attention had belonged to the boys instead of to each other.

They put their ice cream down on the table. "Excuse us," Abby said. "We'll be right back." Her head bobbed up and down. Colette thought she had never seen Abby shake her head so often. It seemed strange, and she wished Abby would stop doing it.

"Don't take too long," warned Ian. "Your ice cream will melt."

The ladies' room in Bailey's was scrungy and smelled of disinfectant. Colette didn't care about the smell. She felt relieved to be alone with Abby. They looked at each other and started to laugh.

"What are we laughing about?" asked Abby.

"I don't know. . . ." Colette was laughing so hard that she snorted. "I know I'm not high. I practically choked on that joint. Were you mad at me for trying it?"

"Are you kidding? I was too chicken-shit. Actually, the only reason I didn't try it at first was that I was scared that you'd be mad at me if I broke the pact."

"And I was the one to break it. I'm sorry."

"Come on, Colette. You hardly ever do anything wrong. Anyhow, forget about the joint. Isn't Abernathy gorgeous? Do you think he likes me?"

"Do you like him?"

Abby pretended to swoon. "What a question! Seriously, what do you think of him?"

Colette hesitated. She couldn't comfortably say that she liked Abernathy. "I wish I could call him Jim. It feels so macho calling him Abernathy."

"He doesn't like the name Jim. He thinks it's too common. Isn't that neat? We have something in common. I don't like my name, either. Abby and Abernathy. It sounds like we go together."

"I like Abby, alone, without the Abernathy. Abby and Abernathy is a mouthful. It'd be tough to make into a song."

Abby looked hurt. "That's not exactly the

sympathy I'm looking for. You aren't jealous, are you?"

Colette shook her head, perhaps just a little too quickly. "No. I'm sorry. It was a feeble joke. Abby and Abernathy will make a great song."

"Forget about a song. Colette, I'm talking about feeling serious about someone for the first time in my life. What am I going to do with him when he tries something? Come on, Colette. A guy like that has obviously got experience. He's going to expect . . . well . . . you know."

"'You know' . . . ?" Colette tried to tease Abby, but then she felt bad. Abby was clearly in no mood for teasing. Besides, part of her *was* jealous. Abernathy did give off a sense of excitement and danger. "I'm sorry, Abb," she said quickly. "What do you want to do with him? I mean, it isn't a sin, whatever it is . . . at least not in our religion."

"What does religion have to do with it?"

"I don't know. It's been on my mind. Does it bother you that they're such Wasps?"

"They're no worse than a lot of the kids at school."

"Well, they go to boarding school. I think they're more super-Waspy than we're used to. It sort of scares me."

"I think you're making it all up. You're not scared of Wasps, you're scared of sex. Me, too. So stop making such a big deal about this Wasp/Jew thing."

"You might be right."

"I *know* I'm right," said Abby decisively. "We're both scared. It's natural. It's the price of being backward."

"We're not so backward."

Abby gave her an amused stare. "Oh, yeah, well what are you going to do with Ian?"

Colette shrugged. Actually, she wished that she was more scared of Ian. She had a feeling that he would leave it up to her to decide how far they went.

"Oh, hell," said Abby. "Maybe Abernathy isn't even attracted to me. He probably doesn't like flat-chested girls. He probably thinks I'm a nerd. Maybe he'll just say good night and that will be that. What about Ian? Does he turn you on? I think he's sweet. Really."

Colette frowned. "Sweet isn't sexy," she said, but then she felt bad. It wasn't that she didn't like Ian, so why did she put him down?

"You two looked so cute together when you were dancing on the street," said Abby. "He's adorable."

"Do you really think so?" Colette asked.

Abby nodded. "I do."

"Come on . . . our ice cream's melting," said Colette.

As they were leaving the ladies' room, Colette watched Abby lick her lips and pinch her cheeks. Colette felt a strong wave of sadness rush through her body, making her feel almost physically sick. Abby was rushing off to a real romance. Even if Abernathy *was* a bastard, Abby at least was wholeheartedly attracted to him. Colette couldn't make herself feel the same way about Ian. She felt too in control.

But when she walked back out and saw Ian looking for her, her mood changed. Seeing Ian made her happy, even if it wasn't thrilling like it was for Abby when she saw Abernathy. Colette ate her ice cream silently while Abby and Abernathy traded animated gossip about the Beatles. Ian had finished his sundae. Colette toyed with the dark, thick fudge on the bottom of her glass.

"I can tell you're the kind who saves the best for last," said Ian.

"I do," said Colette. "I've been that way since I was a little kid. Sometimes it drives Abby crazy because it takes me so long to eat. When our families go out for Chinese food, I have to be careful, because if I wait too long, there isn't any left."

"Well, I never was one to save the best for last," said Ian.

"Well, I guess that's what makes horse races." Colette hoped she wasn't blushing again. She wondered what Ian meant. Perhaps she wouldn't be as much in control as she thought.

"You ready to go?" Ian asked.

Colette nodded. Ian stood up and held her coat for her. This time her arms found the sleeves naturally, and she found she liked the light touch of Ian's hands on her shoulders.

Colette and Abby lived only two blocks from each other, and never had those blocks loomed so large in Colette's mind. As the four of them walked home, she knew that the moment was going to have to arrive when Abernathy and Abby went off together and she was alone with Ian.

"You've gotten awfully quiet," Ian said.

"I'm sorry," said Colette quickly. Then she laughed. "There I go. Do you remember that movie they made a long time ago that was filmed in Cambridge, at Harvard? It was called *Love Story*. The lovers kept telling each other that 'Love means never having to say you're sorry.' Abby and I went together and we sobbed. We've seen it seven times. The girl dies." Colette knew she was babbling again. She wished she could stop.

To her surprise, Ian took her hand. He didn't look at her when he did it, and he kept his eyes averted from hers as they walked. Was he afraid that she would pull away? Actually, Colette liked the feel of his hand. She remembered the first time she had touched his hand at the fair—she had expected it to be sweaty, but it had felt cool and dry.

She liked thinking of how they looked together, walking down Brattle Street. Anyone looking at them would think they were a couple who had known each other for a long time. Abby and Abernathy were behind them, and Colette knew that they would have to notice that she and Ian were holding hands. She was pleased by the image she knew they were seeing.

When they reached Abby's corner, Colette

no longer dreaded it. In fact, she couldn't imagine why she had felt so depressed just moments ago.

"I'll see you back at my house," said Abernathy. "You've got the key, right?"

"Check," said Ian. "We're staying at Abernathy's on Beacon Hill, so we don't have to worry about getting back out to Andover." Colette wondered how many houses Abernathy's family had.

Now that Colette was alone with Ian, her hand cramped in his, but she didn't want to hurt him by pulling away. They walked the remaining two blocks in silence. Colette wished that she could think of something to say. She wished she could think of some questions to ask Ian. The magazines that told you how to talk to boys always said, "ask questions." Well, all the questions that the magazines suggested had flown right out of Colette's head.

"Abernathy always comes on strong," said Ian. "What did you think of him? I hope Abby can handle him."

Colette wished that Ian had thought of something else to talk about. "Abby will be okay," she said.

"It's funny. When I watched you perform, I thought she was tough, but tonight I realized she wasn't."

"What about me? Did you think I was tough?"

Ian shook his head. "No. Your voice is so beautiful. It's strong but not tough."

"We both put on an act when we perform. You should be careful not to take it too seriously. I've got a feeling I'm tougher than you think."

"You're not so tough," said Ian. He put his arms around her and drew her toward him. Colette not only didn't feel tough, she felt a powerful urge to run. She and Ian were nearly the same height. Her eyes had no place to go. She focused on his chin.

"Hey, look at me, tough guy," Ian said. Colette could tell that it was hard for Ian to speak. She raised her eyes. She was surprised at how soft his eyes looked.

"You're not so tough yourself," whispered Colette.

He pulled her closer to him. Their noses bumped. Colette twisted her face just a fraction of an inch, but unfortunately, Ian also moved the same fraction and their noses bumped again. Colette felt a desire to laugh, but she stifled it. Ian held her tighter. This time their noses managed to slip by each other and Ian's lips found hers. Colette felt a little as if they were still acting for the benefit of passersby, but she liked the kiss. His lips were surprisingly firm and experienced. It wasn't a wet or mushy kiss at all, and Ian's hands on her back pressed her tighter.

"Thanks," whispered Ian into her ear.

Colette pulled away just a fraction of an inch. She wished he hadn't thanked her.

Abernathy, she was sure, would never thank anyone for a kiss. Colette wished that Ian would just keep kissing her and never ask her permission.

"Did I do something wrong?" Ian asked.

"Why do you think you did something wrong?" Colette was aware that her voice had risen and that she was using that terrible, clipped, polite voice that made her sound like a prig.

"Because you pulled away. Was something wrong with the kiss? I like you, Colette. I really do."

Colette was shocked that he had the nerve to ask if something was wrong with his kiss. He must have felt as scared as she. "Oh, Ian . . . I like you, too . . . I'm sorry. Whoops, there I go again. Saying 'I'm sorry.' I hate myself when I start to sound all hoity-toity and polite. Until I met you, I never used that voice with anyone except my parents."

"I don't think that makes me feel good."

Colette laughed. "It shouldn't. It doesn't make me feel good, either. How can you like me when I'm so mean to you?"

"You're not that mean."

Colette laughed. She still had her arms around Ian, and she rubbed his back. "I'm not?"

Ian shook his head.

Colette wondered if she should tell him that he was really the first official date she had ever had. Certainly it was her first real kiss. She had kissed in kissing games but not for real.

"Can I see you again this weekend?" asked Ian. "Maybe tomorrow? Only let's just hang out, the two of us, without anyone else. Okay?"

"I don't know. Tomorrow I'm supposed to rehearse with Abby. And I've got homework." Colette couldn't figure out why she had said that. It was true, but she could have made time for Ian. It was as if she were afraid of being alone with him.

"You can't rehearse all day. What if I come over around four? Please?"

Colette nodded. "That would be great." She wondered what would happen. To see Ian alone would be totally different. But how? She was almost sure that they would kiss again.

Colette put her key in the door, half hoping that Ian would ask to come inside, but he didn't. She closed the door behind her, relieved that the living room was dark. Her parents must still be out.

Colette climbed the stairs to her room. She took off her blouse, remembering Abernathy's crack. She glanced at the phone. She wondered what Abby was doing with Abernathy. How far would Abby go? Colette wished something more dramatic had happened with Ian.

Finally she fell asleep, and the phone never rang.

Chapter Five

The next morning, Colette couldn't wait to talk to Abby, but when she called her house, she found out that Abby was still asleep.

"Have her call me as soon as she wakes up," she told Mrs. Klein.

Colette went downstairs for breakfast. Her father was sitting at the kitchen table, sipping coffee and reading the newspaper.

"Good morning, sweetheart," he said in his Humphrey Bogart voice.

Colette kissed him on the cheek, then went to get herself some cereal. Her father had been greeting her with his Humphrey Bogart imitation for years now. She had to admit that sometimes she grew tired of it, but she didn't want to insult her father by telling him that. She knew that he thought it was cute.

Her father put the paper down. "So how was your date last night?" he asked. "Mom said that they were both nice boys."

"They were okay," Colette answered. She looked longingly at the phone, willing it to ring. She wanted to talk to Abby so badly. She knew her father meant well, but he almost never talked to her without teasing, and Colette was not in the mood to be teased at the moment.

"The boys were just okay?" asked her father, in exactly the teasing tone that Colette had learned to dread.

"They were fine," said Colette noncommittally, trying to keep her anger in check. Her father had really done nothing this morning to warrant her feeling so angry at him, but Colette felt ready to explode.

Unfortunately for her father, he couldn't or wouldn't read her mood. He kept up the teasing. "You know, when I was your age, the big, *big* question was would a girl kiss on the first date. I'm sure that's all changed now."

"Dad, stuff it." Colette tried to keep her voice light to match his. Her father had a temper, and Colette had learned that he didn't take to being teased back.

"Stuff it? Is that any way to talk to your old man? I thought we were having a civilized discussion about your date last night." Her father's voice was still teasing, but now there was an edge to it.

"Well, I don't see why I have to tell you every detail about my date." Colette couldn't keep the edge out of her voice. She heard it and hated it, hated it because she knew exactly how her father would react—with his typical teenager speech.

"I'm sorry," he said with exaggerated sarcasm. "I forgot for a moment that I was dealing with a volatile teenager who must be allowed her privacy. Forgive me for thinking we could just talk."

"Oh, Dad, please. . . ." begged Colette, unable to find the words that she wanted to say.

She wished with all her heart that conversations with her father hadn't grown so difficult. They never used to fight the way they did now. When Colette was younger, she used to love her father's corny jokes, loved going to see his favorite old movies with him. They'd had a very special relationship, but lately Colette found herself annoyed with him over the slightest things, and it frightened her.

"Dad, I'm sorry," whispered Colette. Her mind flashed to Ian and all the "I'm sorry"s they'd exchanged the night before.

"Apology accepted," said her father in a tone that Colette knew she was supposed to take as a peace offering. "By the way, I saw in the paper that *A Hard Day's Night* is playing at the Square. It's a wonderful movie. I always loved Ringo in it. Would you like to see it together this afternoon?"

"Oh, Dad, we saw it last night. But Ringo is my date's favorite Beatle, too." Colette felt that giving him that tidbit of information would be her peace offering.

"Well, at least he's got good taste," admitted her father.

Colette took a breath. For the moment, the atmosphere seemed to have calmed down again, but it felt more like a negotiated truce with her father than a true clearing of the air.

"Well, maybe I'll see if your mother wants to go," said her father.

Finally, the phone rang. Colette jumped for it, praying that it was Abby. Luckily, it was.

"Can you come over right away?" Abby asked.

Colette laughed. "Are you kidding? I couldn't wait for you to get up. I'll be there in a second."

Abby giggled. "Oh, I'm so glad. I've got so much to tell you. Hurry."

Colette hung up. She practically flung her cereal bowl into the sink.

"Abby, I presume," said her father.

"Yeah, I'm going over there. We have to practice."

"Somehow, it didn't sound as if you were getting that excited about just practicing. You're going to have some 'girl talk.' Am I right?"

Colette clenched her teeth. She would not, would not, pick a fight with her father. There was nothing wrong with wanting to go over to Abby's. And there was no reason for her to feel so guilty about keeping her personal life to herself. Why did her father have to make her feel like she was abandoning him?

"What are you doing this morning?" she asked.

"Don't worry about me, little one. I have a squash game. Run along to Abby." Her father smiled at her. It was weird to hear him use the same half-teasing endearment that Abernathy had called Abby—"little one."

Abby was still in her nightgown when Colette got to her house. She was playing Go Fish with her younger sister, Dana. "Thank God you're here. I was losing. Come on up to my room."

"That's not fair," complained Dana. "Can't we finish?"

"Later. I've got to talk to Colette."

"You promised."

"Greg!" shouted Abby to her brother. "Come here and play my hand with Dana!"

"I don't want to play with Greg."

"Then play solitaire."

Colette listened to the familiar, good-natured bickering that seemed to go on non-stop in Abby's house.

"Okay, tell me," said Colette when they were finally alone. "Did you kiss him good night? I kissed Ian."

"Did I *kiss* him?" shrieked Abby. "Oh, Colette, I'm in love. I kissed him. He put his tongue in my mouth. Remember when we used to talk about how it was unsanitary and disgusting and we couldn't imagine doing it? Well, it didn't feel like that. It felt weird. But exciting. Oh, God, I think I'm in love. And to think that yesterday at this very moment I didn't even know he existed."

Colette smiled at Abby. She wished with all her heart that she could say she felt the same way about Ian. Abby sounded so happy. It sounded like all the songs they had sung together, but now it was real for Abby.

"How about you?" Abby asked. "Was it wonderful?"

Colette had never lied to Abby. "Well, it was a good kiss. He's a good kisser. I think he's got lots of experience."

"It's fate! We were destined to fall in love with two people who are best friends. Abernathy's a Scorpio—that's a very sexy sign. Since I'm an Aries, we're a very combustible mixture."

"Since when did you start believing in astrology?"

"Well, that's what Abernathy told me."

"Do you call him Abernathy when he's kissing you?"

Abby laughed. "No, I couldn't call him anything. He was holding me so tight, I could hardly breathe. In fact, my lips hurt this morning. Oh, Colette, you don't think we did the wrong thing by letting them kiss us good night, do you? You don't think they'll think we're cheap?"

Colette laughed. "Are you kidding? You sound like my father. Nobody thinks that way anymore. What a double standard! If Ian or Abernathy thought that, I'd give them a punch in the mouth."

"I like Ian," said Abby. "He's easy to talk to."

"Do you find Abernathy easy to talk to?" Colette asked.

Abby hooted. "Who talked? After we left you, we hardly came up for air. He kissed me as soon as you turned the corner, and then he just didn't stop." Abby flung herself on the bed, her arms outspread. *"I love him! I love him!"* she screamed.

Colette smiled, but she felt uncomfortable again. Abby sat up on her bed. "Do you think maybe you're in love with Ian?" she asked.

Colette gave a half-embarrassed shrug. "It's so weird. It wasn't the way you say it was with Abernathy and you. At least not the whole time. We were going along great, and then all of a sudden it was like a monster grew inside me, and Ian couldn't do anything right. I even hated the way he breathed. Then I felt all guilty because he hadn't done anything wrong. Then a couple of minutes later everything was okay again."

"My feelings about Abernathy don't change," said Abby seriously. "I think he's perfect. No, I don't mean exactly perfect, but there's nothing I would change. He's so good-looking."

Colette sighed. If only she was sure about Ian. Abby was lucky. She had no doubts about the way she felt. Colette was on an emotional roller coaster.

Abby started pacing around her room. "Colette, do you realize that this is the first real person I've ever felt anything for? All the crushes I've had, they've never even been on anyone I knew. Don't you think it's a sign of maturity that I've transferred my feelings to a real, sexy person—someone in my life—instead of some rock star?"

Colette nodded, trying hard to curb her jealousy. If only she could have felt that way about Ian. She was worried that she was too cautious and critical. She might never fall in love!

Abby looked serious. "Colette, I'm not kidding about this. I've never felt this way before. It's like all the songs. I feel like I've been hit by lightning. All I can do is think about him."

"I'm glad," said Colette. And she meant it. Abby looked so happy. Colette just wished that she could feel the same way. No doubts. Just pure love!

At four o'clock that afternoon, Ian showed up at Colette's door, carrying a red rose. He handed it to her diffidently. "Corny, huh? But when I was walking from the subway station, I passed a flower store and I wanted to get you one. I realized I had never bought a girl a flower."

Colette smelled the rose. Then she reached over and put her arm around his neck and gave him a kiss on the lips. "No one ever gave me a flower, either. It's a first." She stepped back and noticed that his ears were turning pink.

"Promise you won't take this the wrong way—I'm not saying this to embarrass you— but, you know, the first thing I noticed about you was your pink ears." Colette put her hand over her mouth. How could she have just blurted out the first thing that came to mind? Poor Ian. He'd bought her a lovely flower, and all she could do was tease him. She was worse than her father.

Ian put his hands over his ears. "They turn pink whenever I'm embarrassed, and they stick out, too. I hate them! My mother says that I look like Prince Charles. I went through a stage where I'd tape them down at night in the hopes that they would grow closer to my head."

Colette laughed. "I didn't think boys did things like that."

"Well, I did. I'm glad you mentioned my ears. I always figure girls are looking at them. Now, at least, it's out in the open. So to speak. Of course, with my ears, they're always out in the open."

"I'm glad . . . not about your ears . . . they're fine. But glad you're not mad that I mentioned them, because as soon as I did I was sorry. Whoops, there are the two words we promised we'd try not to say. Anyhow, I don't think you should be self-conscious about them."

Ian groaned. "Sorry, but don't you hate it when you're self-conscious about something and everybody tells you not to be? I mean, it doesn't do you any good. What are you self-conscious about?"

Without realizing what she was doing, Colette glanced down at her breasts. She felt herself turn red. "Well, at least I never taped them down," she said. Then she blushed deeper as Ian laughed. "I don't know what it is with you. I say the queerest things to you. It's like—I don't know."

"Look, do you think I go around telling everyone that I used to tape down my ears?"

Colette shook her head. Just then her father came in the front door, carrying his squash jacket. He did an elaborate double take when he saw Colette with her rose.

"Young maiden with red rose, a very pretty picture." He smiled and held out his hand.

"Hello, I'm Colette's father, Ed. You must be . . ."

"Ian Mitchell, sir." Ian shook his hand vigorously.

"Please, no 'sir.' No, sir, that's my baby . . ." He began to hum and did a little tap dance.

"Dad took tap-dance lessons," explained Colette. "We all did." She felt tender toward her father, even though he was embarrassing her. If only he didn't always have to try so hard.

"Anyhow, call me Ed. If I were twins, you could say two Eds are better than none."

"If you were twins, your brother's name wouldn't likely be Ed, would it?" asked Ian. "I mean, you don't normally give twins the same name, do you?"

Colette's father laughed, to Colette's ears a bit too heartily. "That's right. Very clever of you to point that out. I can see you're not going to have a dull time with Ian, Colette. By the way, what has the dullest life in the house?"

"Daddy," protested Colette, feeling like she wanted to die. But her father plowed on.

"Give up?" he asked Ian.

Ian nodded, seeming to sense how uncomfortable Colette was.

"The bed is the dullest thing in the house because it gets made up every day, but it never goes out."

"That's pretty good . . ." Ian started to say "sir" but stopped himself just in time. He turned to Colette. "Would you like to take a walk?" he asked. "The sun is still warm. We could go down by the river."

Colette nodded quickly. "I'll just put the rose in a vase." She left the room, feeling uneasy about leaving Ian alone with her father. But when she returned with the rose in a bud vase, her father and Ian were sitting in the living room, seemingly having a comfortable conversation.

Ian stood up when Colette entered. Why did he have to be so damn polite all the time? Colette got her jacket and they went outside. She felt as if a weight was lifted when they shut the front door behind them. The wind was cool, and the grass was already covered with falling leaves. Her annoyance vanished.

"Your father's a nice guy. I didn't realize he was a professor."

"I'm sorry about all his bad jokes. I think he's shy sometimes, like me, and he tries to make up for it with my friends by telling all these horrendous jokes."

"That's not the worst crime in the world."

"I know. But sometimes parents can be a pain. You're lucky to go to boarding school. You escape."

"From some things, yeah. But look, my Dad tells bad jokes, too. He can be pompous. Let's not talk about parents. It's depressing." They walked down Brattle Street past the Mormon church which was across the street from Longfellow's house. The Divinity School was on their left.

"Cambridge sure is full of churches," said Ian.

"Well, the Puritan influence and all that."
Colette tried to make a joke, but it came out
lame. Why did her father have to make such
an ass out of himself? He had been even more
awkward than usual. Was it because he was
awed by Ian's upper-class manners? Colette
knew that her father sometimes felt intimi-
dated by Wasps. He spoke of it often, always
making jokes about it.

Colette wondered if Ian knew she was
Jewish. Gordon was such a nondescript
name. She wished she knew how she felt
about being Jewish. Did going out with Ian
mean she had to take sides? Why had she
made that stupid joke about the "Puritan
influence"? She'd like to stay far away from
the subject of religion.

Ian seemed as uncomfortable with the subject as she was. "Well, I'm not feeling puri-
tanical today," he said with a sort of fake
laugh. He took her hand. They crossed the
park and walked along the path beside the
Charles River. Colette liked holding Ian's
hand. She smiled at him, but still she felt
shy. She couldn't think of anything to say.

"Did Abby have a good time last night?"
Ian asked.

Colette nodded. She felt protective of Abby.
"Did Abernathy?"

"Abernathy . . . He always has a good
time. You don't have to worry about him. I
just hope Abby doesn't get hurt."

Colette hesitated. "Abby thinks she's in
love with Abernathy." Colette just blurted
out the words.

"Uh oh."

"What exactly does that mean?" asked Colette, sorry now that she had told Ian how Abby felt.

"Well, I don't think Abernathy is the greatest person for Abby to fall in love with."

"I didn't think so, either, but I couldn't tell her that."

"Why not?"

"I just couldn't. She really, really cares for him. Abby and I never tell each other what to do. That's why we're such good friends. You'll have to make sure that he doesn't hurt her."

Ian looked worried. "I can't do that. Nobody can make Abernathy do anything. People have been trying all his life."

"Well, I don't know," said Colette, exasperated. "Why does everything have to be so God-awful complicated?"

"It doesn't," said Ian. "At least not between us. None of this has much to do with us."

Colette swallowed. She knew Ian was going to kiss her again, and the knowledge made her nervous. Ian's hands fumbled as he put his arms around her neck. He pulled her closer. This time, when they kissed, Colette opened her mouth slightly to see if Ian would do anything. His tongue pushed against her teeth. It felt alive, but certainly not unsanitary or disgusting. It was thrilling to feel something that alive in her own mouth. It felt so different from her own tongue.

Then, quickly, Ian's tongue was gone, but

he continued to kiss her. Ian opened his own
mouth, and Colette explored it with her
tongue. The inside of his mouth was smooth
and slippery and her tongue was full of
sensations that sent waves all through her
body. The kiss seemed to take forever, and
Colette was willing for it to go on and on. She
wondered if they were going for some kind of
record.

Finally they paused, moving their lips
apart. Colette took a deep breath. Ian smiled
at her. He wore a self-satisfied grin, as if they
had both just accomplished an athletic feat,
like running the mile in a record high school
time. Colette realized she was grinning back.
She had passed a milestone. Her first rose
and her first tongue-in-mouth kiss—all in
the same day. Her life was looking up.

Chapter Six

Colette didn't see Ian again for nearly two weeks. He had midterms, and he had to study, but he called often. Unfortunately, Abernathy didn't call Abby. Finally Ian's midterms were over and he called Colette on a Thursday night. "I think I aced Latin," he said smugly. "Let's celebrate."

"What do you have in mind?"

Ian gave what he obviously hoped was a wicked laugh. "I will hold you down and tickle you until you beg for mercy."

"I hate to be tickled."

"Okay, I'll think of something else. Seriously. I've missed you. Can I come in on Saturday and just spend some time with you, alone?"

Colette hesitated. Abby was miserable because Abernathy hadn't called her. She had begged Colette to ask Ian if Abernathy had lost her number, but Colette had been too embarrassed to ask.

"What's wrong?" asked Ian. "Don't you want to see me?"

"No . . . I mean, yes. It's just Abby."

"Look, I like Abby, but sometimes three's a crowd."

"How's Abernathy?"

Ian groaned. "Shit," he whispered.

"What does that mean?"

"Nothing. He's been busy. I'll try to fix Abby up with someone better. If that's the only way I can see you."

"Don't sound that way. And besides, Abby doesn't want anyone better. She wants him."

Colette could hear Ian sigh. "I should never have fixed them up in the first place."

"Is Abernathy going with someone else?"

"No."

Colette was surprised by Ian's curtness. "Look, forget I asked."

"Don't get mad at me. All I want to do is to see you. Saturday."

"Fine."

"You don't sound very happy about it."

"I'm happy. Okay?"

"Sound a little happier, please, just for me."

Colette giggled. "Happy . . . happy."

"That's better. A little silly but better. Seriously, let's not make any plans. It'll be just the two of us. We'll just relax. Okay?"

"Okay." Colette hung up the phone, feeling guilty. She wished that there was some way that she could make Ian force Abernathy to call Abby.

Colette felt restless, wondering what it would be like with Ian tomorrow. She decided to take a bath. She ran steaming hot water into the tub and lowered herself into it.

Colette sucked on an end of the washcloth. Her father always wondered why the ends of their washcloths looked like rags. It was a habit that Colette couldn't stop. She found it comforting.

The water was just starting to turn cool when Colette heard the phone ring. Her mother knocked on the door. "Colette, it's Abby. Do you want to call her back?"

Colette took the washcloth out of her mouth.

"No, Ma, I'll get it."

"Good. She said it was absolutely, positively essential she talk to you."

Colette wrapped a towel around her body and rushed out of the bathroom. "If Abby said it was so important, how come you didn't tell me right away?"

"Abby always sounds that way."

Colette rushed around her mother and dashed into her bedroom, closing the door firmly behind her.

"Abb? . . . What's up? Mom said you said it was important. Is something wrong?"

"Nothing . . . Nothing! Everything is absolutely wonderful. He finally called. He called! We're going with you this weekend."

"Going with us? What are you talking about?"

"Aren't you seeing Ian this weekend?"

"Well, yeah. We were just going to hang around. But he didn't say anything about Abernathy."

"Who cares? Oh, Colette, I feel like jumping out of my skin! I'm so happy."

"That's sensational," said Colette quickly. "Oh, I'm so glad! And it'll be great. Ian and he must have just talked about our all doing something together."

"We're going up to Abernathy's house in Manchester. The four of us. Doesn't that sound wonderful? Oh, my God, Colette, he called! He said he had been studying so hard, he couldn't call before. When he studies, he just goes into intensive overdrive and he can't think of anything else. That's understandable. He's very intense, and you said that they had midterms. That's why you didn't see Ian last weekend. And that's why I didn't see him. So we're even sort of even."

Colette loved hearing Abby sound so happy again. If Abby was happy, then she had a right to be and have a good time with Ian. It made things so much more simple. "Tell me about this plan to go to Manchester. They must have just made it because I talked to Ian a little while ago, and he didn't say anything about it."

"You and I will take the train, and we'll meet the guys there. Oh please, please, say you'll do it . . . because if you and Ian aren't there, maybe it won't work out. You've got to come."

"It sounds great. It'll be romantic," said Colette. "We can walk on the beach. It'll be empty this time of year."

Abby was silent, which Colette knew wasn't like her. "I'm lying," she said. "I'm sorry."

"Lying about what?" Colette felt a terrible

sinking feeling. She knew that Abby had been feeling crazy that Abernathy hadn't called, but what would she lie about? Colette couldn't imagine.

"Well, he wanted me to go to Manchester with him for the day, but I lied and said that you and Ian had invited me to spend the day with you and we should all go together. Colette, I'm scared to spend the whole day alone with him. He hadn't called me in two weeks, and he wanted me to go alone with him to Manchester. I said I'd only go if you and Ian were going."

Colette pulled a pillow from her bed and lay down on her stomach. "I understand that. It's sort of the same with me. I was looking forward to seeing Ian. He wanted to spend the day alone with me, but I was scared, too. This will be much more fun."

"Oh, I hope so. It was weird when he called. I had been waiting for it so long, then when he really was there on the phone, I got all clammy. I just lied without thinking and then I lied to you."

"I don't care about the lie. You didn't really lie to me, Abb. A twenty-second lie doesn't count."

"I know. We'll make a new pact, never to lie to each other for more than twenty seconds. We'll have a twenty-second lie gong."

"Abb, I love you, you know."

Abby laughed. "I know. Now, if only I could get him to say those words."

They both laughed and hung up.

Ian called Colette back a few minutes later.

"You work fast," said Colette. "I heard Abernathy called Abby."

Ian grunted.

"Do you want me to say 'thank you'?"

Ian laughed. "Don't thank me. I'm not sure Abby should thank me."

"What does that mean?"

"Nothing," said Ian. "Forget it."

"Well, I want to know," insisted Colette. "Did you get Abernathy to call Abby?"

"Let's just say that I gave him a push in that direction. But I told you. Nobody *gets* Abernathy to do anything."

Colette hesitated. "Well, I think it's good news, anyhow. No matter how it happened."

"It wasn't exactly all my idea. Is it okay if we meet up at Manchester? It's an easy drive for us from here."

"It sounds like fun."

"You don't mind?" he asked. Colette thought she detected a feeling of disappointment in his voice.

"Of course not," she said, but after she hung up she wondered.

The next morning was a beautiful Indian summer day, with the temperatures in the seventies. Colette was glad now that they had plans to go to the country. She was excited as the train pulled out of the station.

Manchester was about an hour's train ride from Cambridge. Abby was so excited to be seeing Abernathy again that she was practically jumping out of her skin. "Do you think we'll meet his parents? What if they don't like me? Do you think I should have gotten dressed up?"

Abby was wearing jeans and a long-sleeved purple T-shirt with glitter buttons around the neck. Colette thought she looked wonderful.

"You're lucky you don't feel so passionate about Ian," said Abby. "It must be much more calming."

"Thanks."

"Oh, I didn't mean it that way, Colette. I'm sorry. I'm just nervous. You've been talking to Ian almost every night. It's like you know him now, but Abernathy is still a mystery to me."

"Ian is sort of a mystery to me, too," said Colette. "I don't know him all that well."

Ian and Abernathy were waiting for them at the Manchester train station. They were sitting on the hood of a bright red Pontiac Trans-Am. Ian jumped off when he spotted them, but Abernathy stayed on the hood and waited.

"You made it," Ian said, self-consciously, since it was obvious they were there. He seemed nervous.

"Hi, Ian," shouted Abby. "We made it." She gave him a big hug, as if they were the oldest friends in the world.

Abernathy rolled off the hood of his car and leaned against it. Behind him, in the distance, Colette could see the masts of sailboats bobbing in the harbor.

"Hi, Colette." Abernathy held his hand out to her. Abby stood at Colette's side, shuffling her feet. Then she sort of lunged at Abernathy, who caught her.

"Hi, little one. Welcome to Manchester."

They piled into the car—Abby and Abernathy in front, Colette and Ian in back. Colette realized that this was yet another first, her first drive with someone her own age. Abernathy put a cassette in the tape deck and blasted it loud. A group of kids hanging around in the parking lot turned to stare at them.

Abernathy gunned the engine. He accelerated, and Colette was thrown back in the car seat. Ian caught her and put his arm around her shoulder. Colette was worried; ever since she was a little girl she'd had bouts of carsickness.

Up in the front seat, Abby sat close to Abernathy. They turned onto a narrow road, which Colette noticed with misgivings was called Cliff Road. "Is it far?" she shouted.

Abernathy turned in his seat. "What did you say?"

"I asked if your house is far. Cliff Road sounds a little scary." Ian squeezed her shoulder. Colette swallowed. She hoped she wouldn't throw up. She felt she'd die of embarrassment if she did.

"The house is right here," said Ian. They pulled into the driveway of a large white house that was surrounded by giant pine trees. The house had a deserted air to it, and the driveway was empty. The garage doors were locked tight.

"We're here," said Ian.

Colette stumbled out of the car.

"This is a beautiful house," said Abby. "Sensational. Can you see the water from the other side?"

"Why do you think they call it Cliff Road? We're right on a cliff overlooking the sea. Come on in," said Abernathy.

They went into the house, which seemed lonesome and airless. Cotton sheets were draped over the furniture, and all the blinds were drawn. The house was huge. It seemed much too large to be used just for summer vacations.

"It looks like a ghost house," said Colette, trying to make a joke about the sheets on the furniture. But she felt as if the joke sounded lame. She turned around. Ian and Abernathy were each carrying two heavy-looking bags of groceries.

"Supplies," said Ian. He pulled out two six packs of beer. Abernathy had another two six packs and bags of tortilla chips and Cheese Puffs. He snapped the lid open on one of the cans and handed it to Abby. She took a sip. Ian handed Colette a can and opened one for himself.

Colette watched as Ian took a long sip. Thirsty from the train, she took a sip, too. It tasted good. Her father drank a lot of beer, so she was used to the taste. She began to relax. Being alone in the house was exciting. It felt sophisticated to be drinking beer in the middle of the afternoon. She moved to the window, pulled aside the heavy, flowered drapes, and looked down across the lawn to the sea.

"Can you get to the beach from here?" Colette asked.

"Sure. There are steps to the boat house down the cliff. We'll all go," said Ian. They walked out into the sunshine.

Outside, Abernathy grabbed Abby's hand and they ran across the lawn. Ian caught up with Colette. "You seem tense. Is something wrong? You don't mind about the beer, do you?"

What kind of a prude did he think she was? She took another sip of her beer. She wanted to tell him that she felt out of place, out of her element. Abernathy's house had an unfriendly feel to it. It was so spacious and neat, so unlike her own cozy, cluttered home. The beer didn't bother Colette, the place did.

"Well, what's wrong?" Ian repeated.

Colette didn't answer. "Nothing's wrong," she said finally, but as soon as she said it, she realized she was lying. She felt awful. She didn't feel rejected by the house, she felt rejected by Ian. True, he had done nothing to make her feel that way. Perhaps her feelings were irrational, but she felt wrong for the house, wrong for him! Ian seemed like a stranger, and a stranger who thought he was superior to her at that.

All the ease and pleasure she had gotten from their telephone calls had disappeared. Ian was a different person now. There he was, sipping his beer, acting so proud of himself for nothing, for having a friend who had a big empty house where you could take girls.

"Nothing's wrong," repeated Colette miserably. She told herself to stop acting like such a pill. Why couldn't she be happy? It would be normal to be happy. This was exactly what she had been longing for ever since she was young. She and Abby would find two guys. They would begin finally to live life, instead of just singing about it. It was a beautiful Indian summer day. She was in a huge mansion with a boy. What more could she want? How could any sane person be miserable on such a day?

"I'm sorry," said Colette.

Ian shook his head. "We haven't been together five minutes and already you're saying, 'I'm sorry.'"

"Well, I'm sorry for my 'I'm sorries.'" Colette started to laugh. She sounded so stupid.

Ian took another sip from his beer and then crushed the aluminum can in his hand. He tossed it on the lawn. "Wait here and I'll get another one before we go down to the beach."

"Are you just going to leave it there?" Colette pointed to the beer can.

"I'll pick it up later. Don't worry, there're no litter laws here."

"But it's rude to just leave it on the lawn."

"Colette, I think I know how to behave at Abernathy's house," said Ian in a slightly prissy voice.

Colette refused to look at him. Was he

implying that she didn't know how to behave? She looked ahead. Abby and Abernathy had disappeared down the steps.

"Do you want another beer?" Ian asked.

Colette shook her head. "No, I haven't even finished this one. You can have it."

"Are you sure?"

"Sure." She shoved it at him. The afternoon stretched ahead endlessly. Colette wished Abby hadn't gone off with Abernathy.

Ian took the beer can from her. "Isn't it beautiful here? We go sailing from the harbor. It's one of the best harbors in New England, but tricky. Do you sail?"

"No. I get seasick," snapped Colette, imitating Ian's prissy voice. The truth was that she had never been sailing.

"You don't have to snap my head off. I'm sorry you get seasick."

"I'm sorry if I offended you because I don't sail," Colette said, clipping off each word.

"Christ," said Ian. "Who cares if you sail?"

"You do, evidently," said Colette, knowing that she was escalating this argument to a ridiculous level. Ian clearly didn't care if she sailed or not.

"You're crazy, you know that? I don't know what we're arguing about."

"You would prefer a girl who sails. I can tell."

Ian grabbed her. "You are driving me nuts."

Colette began to giggle.

"Oh, shit, Ian. I'm sorry. I didn't mean it. If 'love is never having to say you're sorry,' I'm a complete screw-up at it." She relaxed against his chest. She looked up and to her surprise saw that Ian looked honestly upset.

"You scared me," he said softly. "I don't understand why it got so terrible here all of a sudden."

"I don't, either," said Colette. "It's like I can't stop myself."

Ian held her. His hands rubbed her back and her shoulders. Then they moved down to the small of her back. Her sweater rode up, and she felt his touch on her bare back. His hands were cold. She flinched.

"I'm sorry," he said.

"There we go again. Your hands feel good. It's just that they're cold."

"Promise you won't go crazy on me like that again," Ian said.

Colette nodded. "I think being in Abernathy's big house kind of freaked me," she admitted.

"Why should a house freak you? It's just a house."

"It's a big house. It just seems so rich."

"Abernathy *is* rich," said Ian matter-of-factly.

"And Waspy," muttered Colette.

"What does that have to do with anything?"

"Well, it's everything I'm not."

"Thank God."

"Why do you say that?" Colette asked.

"I wouldn't want you to be like a house. Built like one, maybe."

Colette shoved him.

"That was just a joke," said Ian quickly.

"It wasn't very funny."

"I know." Ian looked embarrassed. "It was like something dumb out of a tasteless joke book. Honest, I don't usually make tasteless jokes."

"Well, it wasn't so bad, for a tasteless joke. I guess some girls would be flattered."

"I meant it as a compliment. It's weird; I think that maybe I'm just nervous about finally being with you in person. We talked on the phone so much, I got to feeling really easy with you. And now when I'm with you in person, it just feels awkward."

"For me, too," Colette admitted. She lifted her head. "I know a way we can make it less awkward, Ian."

"How?"

Colette kissed him, pulling him close to her. They kissed for a long time, and their bodies pulled even tighter together. Ian's hands slipped under her sweater and touched the back of her bra.

When they finally broke apart, Ian blinked. He looked worried. Colette realized that he was more than a little bit scared, too. It made her feel wonderful. She touched his eyelashes lightly with her finger, a gesture she had never seen anyone else do before. She felt like she had just invented something, and it made her feel proud.

Chapter Seven

A few minutes later, Abernathy and Abby appeared from the beach. Abernathy grinned at them. He had his hand underneath Abby's sweater. "It's cold down there. We came back up for some warmth."

Abby's teeth were chattering. "I should have brought a jacket. It was so hot in Cambridge."

"What you need is a chamois shirt from L. L. Bean," said Abernathy. "I'll get you one as a present."

Abby smiled at Colette. Colette could understand why Abby was so happy. It wasn't really the present that thrilled Abby; Abernathy had implied that they had a future. Abernathy had won her just by the simple use of the future tense. He was going to buy her a present at some future date.

However, his next words changed everything. "Let's go get one now. Maine is just a couple of hours away. We could get there and pick you up a shirt. Let's go."

"Wait a minute," said Colette. "We can't just go to Maine."

"Why not? You don't need a passport." Abernathy laughed. "Besides, you and Ian can sit in the backseat. We won't bother you."

"It'll be fun," said Ian. "It's a beautiful day for a ride."

Abby laughed. "Okay, we'll go to Maine." She grinned at Colette. "Think of it this way, it'll be an adventure. We wanted an adventure and now we've got it."

Abby took Colette's arm. "I just hope I don't get carsick," Colette whispered.

They walked into the empty house. Ian went to the bathroom, leaving Colette alone with Abernathy and Abby. Abernathy picked up the car keys. "Don't worry," said Abby. "It'll be okay."

"I think worrying comes naturally to Colette," said Abernathy. "It seems to be her style. You and Ian are suited to each other. He's a worrier, too."

"Stop riding her," said Abby. "She's not a worrier—at least not much."

"I wasn't riding her," said Abernathy. "You know, Colette, Abby worries about you a lot. You two always stick together, and you're so quick on the draw about each other. Ian was right."

"Right about what?" Colette asked.

"Just that it's dangerous to date friends. They always compare notes."

"You guys are much worse gossips than we are," said Abby.

Colette liked it when Abby talked back to Abernathy. She sounded more like herself, less like a wimp. And Abernathy seemed to like Abby better when she mocked him.

Ian came back into the room. "Let's go," said Abernathy, "before the girls change their minds."

Once again Colette and Ian sat in the

backseat of the car. Ian kept his arm around her, but mostly he talked to Abby in the front seat. The two of them chatted as if they had known each other forever. Colette stared out the window, feeling panicked. She wished she hadn't agreed to go. What if she got carsick? She'd ruin the trip for everybody. Besides, there was something a little bit frightening about just picking up and taking off for Maine. Abernathy had drunk a few beers. What if they ended up being a teenage drunk-driving statistic?

"How far is it again?" Colette asked.

"That's the worrier," said Abernathy. "I thought you were being awfully quiet. Maybe I'll buy you a chamois shirt, too."

"No, thanks."

"What's the matter, don't you like the preppy look?" Abernathy asked. "L. L. Bean is too preppy for words."

Colette knew that L. L. Bean was the world's most preppy store. She and Abby had always prided themselves on avoiding the preppy look. She could understand Abby wanting a shirt from Abernathy, but she didn't want him to buy her one, too. That would make Abby's shirt so much less special.

As they drove, Colette began to feel more and more anxious. She found it hard to think of anything to talk about. They drove through perfect little New England towns, each one with a big white church in the center. Colette thought that the towns looked

too white, too proper. They were as unwel-
coming as Abernathy's house.

Once they were on the expressway, Colette
became less nervous. She rarely got carsick
on expressways, just on small back roads.
She decided that even if she were having
trouble talking, it was kind of fun to be in a
car, driving away. No one, not even her
parents, knew where she was. It was scary
but fun.

Ian stopped talking to Abby. He stroked
Colette's hair. She put her head on his chest
and looked up at him. "I can hear your heart
beating. I've never heard anyone's heart before."

Ian smiled at her. "Well, at least you know
I'm not a zombie."

"I never thought you were a zombie."

"I thought maybe you did. 'Cause you
weren't talking."

"Shh . . ." whispered Colette. "I've got to
listen." She put her ear to Ian's chest. The
heartbeat was soft, not a *thunk, thunk,* but a
gentle sound. She felt as if she were eaves-
dropping on his insides. It was strange to
know that her own heart probably sounded
much like Ian's. His hand gently stroked her
wrist, touching the bare skin that showed
just where her shirt ended. He kissed her
hair. Colette opened her eyes. She could feel
her body relax. The music from the tape deck
filled the car as if they were an air bubble in
space. What a joy to be able to get into a car
and drive! Colette understood why Aber-

nathy had the urge just to get behind the
wheel. Why *not* go to Maine?

"Let me listen to your heartbeat," said Ian.

Colette sat up, and Ian put his ear to her
chest. Colette felt her nipples get hard. Ian
kept his head on her chest.

"You've got a good heartbeat," he said.

Colette laughed softly. "Thanks. Nobody
ever said that to me before."

"Well, I'm glad I'm the first. I congratulate
you on a terrific heartbeat. I just think I'll
listen all the way to Maine."

Colette giggled. Abby turned around in the
front seat and saw Ian with his head on
Colette's chest. "Whoops, sorry," she said.
"Didn't mean to intrude."

"We're just conducting scientific experi-
ments back here," said Ian.

"Playing doctor, huh?" asked Abernathy,
glancing into the backseat. Colette wished
that he would keep his eyes on the road. She
felt embarrassed now that Abby and Abernathy were talking to them.

"Sit up," she whispered to Ian.

Ian cocked his eyebrows at her. "But I'm in
the middle of a beat," he protested.

Colette tried to push him up, but Ian lay
down on her lap, like a little baby. "No . . . I
want to stay where I am."

"Come on, Ian, get up. You're being silly."

"Hey, is the backseat getting silly?" said
Abernathy. "If it is, I might want someone
else to drive."

"Mind your own business," said Colette.

"I'm sorry," said Abernathy. "Are we disturbing you two?"

"Yeah," said Ian. "As a matter of fact. Why doesn't the front seat mind its own business?"

Colette bit her lip. She didn't want Abby to be hurt. "No, it's okay. The front seat doesn't have to mind its own business."

Ian stared at her.

"How far away is L. L. Bean really?" Colette asked.

"About a hundred miles," said Abernathy.

Suddenly what they were doing hit Colette. "A hundred miles! We won't get back till late. I promised my parents we'd be home before ten tonight. We'd better not be too late."

"I remember meeting your parents," said Abernathy. "Your mom wasn't uptight at all. We'll just call them and tell them you're spending the night in Manchester. What's the problem?"

"Right," said Ian. "It's a big house. No problem."

Suddenly the whole thing felt crazy. "Abby, we're nuts. We can't go to Maine. Our parents will kill us. What are we doing?"

"Can't you stop her from being so uptight?" Abernathy asked Abby.

Abby shot Colette a worried look. "Come on, we're all together. And I bet if we call our folks and tell them we're spending the night together, it'll be okay. They don't have to know Abernathy's parents aren't there."

Ian squeezed Colette's hand. She didn't

want him to worry about her, to think she was such a prude that she couldn't handle an adventure. And as long as she was with Abby, Colette decided she didn't have to worry. The only problem was that her mind seemed to have a worry button of its own. She was frightened of the idea of lying to her parents and spending the night in that spooky house with sheets all over the furniture.

Colette inched over to the window.

"Don't worry," said Ian. "It'll be okay."

Colette glanced over at him. She wondered what he expected would happen if they all spent the night together. Ian still had her hand in his. He stretched his arm. He flexed his fingers. "My hand fell asleep."

"Sorry," said Colette.

"Don't let's start that again!"

"What's that, an inside joke?" Abby asked.

Ian nodded, looking smug. Colette was embarrassed. Ian was bragging that he had a history with Colette almost as close and secretive as her life with Abby. Colette thought that his smile looked insecure and nervous, and she was sure that Abby had noticed that he was laughing too loudly.

Colette rolled the window down. "Is something wrong, Colette?" Abby asked. "You're not carsick, are you?"

"Don't tell me she gets carsick, too!" said Abernathy.

"Don't worry Abernathy, I won't throw up all over your precious car."

"Are you kidding? The vomit this car has seen would fill buckets. Right, Ian? Some of it is yours."

"This conversation is disgusting," said Abby. "I don't want to hear any more."

"Better to hear about it than smell it," said Ian. "Remember the night we went to the country club with a bottle of vodka disguised in one of those big plastic Coke bottles, and we drank it all? Boy, was I blotto."

"Yeah, that's when the backseat really got it," said Abernathy.

"It's real cute listening to the two of you talk about throwing up," said Colette. "Can't we change the subject? If I get carsick, it won't be funny."

"Let's talk about something else," said Abby, for Colette's sake.

"Why don't you two sing something," said Ian. "I love to listen to you."

"Okay," said Abby. "But you have to sing, too. You too, Abernathy."

They sang some Police songs, and Michael Jackson, but Colette and Abby were the only ones who knew all the words. Then they turned to stupid songs from camp. They sang "Michael Row the Boat Ashore," "This Land Is Your Land," and "I Know an Old Lady Who Swallowed a Fly." Ian knew most of the words. Even Abernathy began to sing along. Colette snuggled back on the seat. She liked the feel of Ian's arm around her, holding her tight, making her feel secure.

She liked the feeling of being free in a car. No adults. No restraints. Free.

Chapter Eight

It was almost dark when they drove into the L. L. Bean parking lot. The store was famous for being open twenty-four hours a day, three hundred and sixty four days a year. It only closed for twelve hours on Christmas day.

"I can remember when only a few people knew about L. L. Bean," said Abernathy, sounding as if he were forty years old. "It used to be a well-kept secret. Hunters and fishermen would stop here at dawn. Then *The Preppy Handbook* and that parody, *Items From Our Catalog,* made L. L. Bean a cliché."

It was Colette's first visit ever to Maine. The store looked small compared to what she had expected, but then they went inside and she realized that its size was deceptive. In fact, the store was enormous. Colette stared at everything on the ground floor. It was filled with canoes and camping equipment. It looked as if an army could bivouac there.

As Colette looked around, she made up her mind to buy Ian a present. Why should Abernathy be the only one who got to feel good about himself for giving a gift? And *her* present would be a surprise. She wondered what she could buy him that he would like and that she could afford.

"Come on," said Abernathy. "I know this store really well."

"You all go ahead," said Colette. "I'll catch up with you. I have to go to the bathroom."

"Want me to come with you?" asked Abby.

Abernathy had his arm around Abby's waist. "No, enough of you two always running off together. Remember, the whole point of this trip was to get you a shirt."

"Go ahead, Ian," said Colette. "You go with them. I'll meet you by the shirts."

"It's right over there," said Abernathy, pointing across the vast room.

As soon as she was alone, Colette backtracked to a counter where she had seen a pair of maroon earmuffs in a beautiful fuzzy material. She picked them up. She loved them. She would get them for Ian. She just hoped he wouldn't think that she was making fun of his ears.

She was pleased to find out that the earmuffs weren't too expensive. "I'll take them," said Colette. "Quickly. I don't want my friend to see them. They're a surprise."

She gave the clerk the money and put the earmuffs in her purse, feeling terrific. It was fun to buy Ian a present.

Colette almost skipped across the floor to the clothing department. Ian smiled at her when she got there, but Abby and Abernathy were deep in conversation. Several chamois shirts in different colors were lying on the counter. Abernathy held a navy one next to Abby's face.

"I never wear navy," complained Abby. "Don't they have it in purple?"

"Purple is a JAP color," said Abernathy. "You wear too much of it."

A Jewish American Princess! Abby! Colette heard Ian take a sharp breath. Abby looked as if she had been slapped across the face. Even the salesperson looked embarrassed.

"Hey, watch your mouth, Abernathy," said Ian angrily.

Abernathy started to laugh nervously. "Honest, Abby, I didn't mean anything. I'm sorry."

He sounded whiny and suddenly very young. Abby put the navy chamois shirt back on the glass counter. "Forget it," she said.

Ian looked at Colette as if he expected her to tell him what to do. She was proud of him for reacting strongly. Abernathy was a creep after all! Her suspicions about him were right. He was an upper-class snob. But Ian wasn't!

"Abby?" said Abernathy. "Can I talk to you alone?"

"It's not such a big deal." mumbled Abby. "After all, purple probably is a JAP color."

"Stop putting yourself down, Abby," said Ian. "Abernathy should learn when to keep his big mouth shut."

Abernathy shot Ian a dirty look. "Abby, may I *please* speak to you alone?"

Abby nodded, then gave Colette a helpless look.

Abernathy took her across the floor where they stood under a hanging row of down sleeping bags. Abby looked tiny standing beneath them. Colette wondered what they were saying.

"I'm sorry," said Ian. "Sometimes Abernathy doesn't think before he opens his mouth."

"Don't apologize for him," said Colette. "I thought it was terrific the way you stood up for Abby."

"Well, I like her, and I hate it when he puts her down. But you should talk to Abby. You shouldn't let her put herself down. I know that kind of humor is supposed to be funny—look at Woody Allen. But Abby does it too much. Even if she's Jewish, it's not funny."

Colette felt a queasy feeling in her stomach. *Even?*

"Ian, you know I'm Jewish, too," Colette said.

"Come on," said Ian. "That's not funny."

"I'm not being funny. It's the truth."

He stared at her. "You don't look Jewish. You don't act Jewish."

"What is that supposed to mean? Who acts Jewish?"

Ian looked at her closely. "Are you putting me on?"

Colette shook her head angrily.

"Well, it doesn't make any difference to me," said Ian. "That's why I got so mad at Abernathy." His voice sounded tight and nervous. Colette wished they were anywhere but standing in the middle of L. L. Bean. She wished with all her heart that she wasn't so far away from home.

Just then Abby and Abernathy came back. Abernathy had his arm resting on Abby's shoulder. "Colette," he said. "Abby has accepted my official apology. I hope you will forgive me, too. I mean it. I'm not joking around. Ian was right. It was a stupid remark to make. I'm sorry."

"He really means it," said Abby so quickly that Colette felt for her.

"You don't have to apologize to me," said Colette.

"I don't have to, but I want to," said Abernathy in a voice more sincere and less affected than Colette had ever heard from him. Colette looked at him. His long eyelashes were actually batting up and down, but out of nervousness, and not for effect.

Abernathy looked down at Abby. "Little one, can I still buy you a shirt?" He grinned at her. Colette still didn't trust him. She didn't like this quick turnaround. His apology seemed too easy.

"Purple?" asked Abby.

Colette tried to laugh, but she was still upset about her unfinished conversation with Ian.

"Purple," agreed Abernathy.

He pulled out a charge card and handed it to the salesperson. Colette had never known anyone her own age who had charge cards in their own name.

"Would you like a purple chamois shirt, too?" Ian asked. "You were wearing a purple blouse the night we first went out."

"I remember." Colette thought about it.

Should she still be angry at Ian? And for what? Because he thought she didn't look Jewish? Colette knew that she didn't look Jewish. It wasn't Ian's fault. But she felt torn. Suddenly the whole idea of the presents had gotten soiled. She thought about the earmuffs in her purse and felt like throwing them away.

"Please, Colette. I'd like to buy you one," said Ian. "It would be a memento of our trip."

"Oh, get one, Colette," said Abby. "We can wear them together on stage. Maybe we can start calling ourselves the Chamois."

"I'd really like to buy you one," said Ian.

No man other than her father had ever bought her a piece of clothing. Colette looked at Ian's face. He looked so eager to please her.

"I'd love one," she said.

She was embarrassed when she had to tell the salesperson that she took a shirt in a size twelve, two sizes larger than Abby.

"Let's put them on right now," said Abby. "Come on, Colette, let's go to the dressing room."

"Yeah, you girls go put on the shirts," said Abernathy. "We'll meet you on the main floor, by the entrance. There's something else I want to check out as long as we're here, okay?" Again Abernathy looked younger and less sure of himself. He seemed to wait for Abby's approval. On the other hand, Colette thought that Abby looked older, more mature. It was as if the balance of power had shifted. Now Abby suddenly looked like she was becoming a woman, and Abernathy, who looked so manly, had returned to being a young boy.

Colette and Abby stood side by side in the tiny dressing room.

"Are you okay?" Abby asked. "You seem upset. Did that JAP comment really bother you?"

"Didn't it bother you?"

"Yeah, but I think it was sort of neat that he apologized so quickly. You can't hold it against him." Abby's voice sounded shaky.

"Ian didn't know I was Jewish," Colette blurted out.

"Did you tell him?"

"Of course, and he made a big deal about how it didn't matter to him. As if he were doing me a favor!"

"Don't be so hard on him. Ian really likes you, I can tell."

Colette sat down on a tiny triangular bench in the dressing room. She held her purple chamois shirt between her knees. "I feel like telling them both to go to hell."

Abby stared at her. "I think you're overreacting."

Colette put her arm in the sleeve of the shirt. The material was stiffer than she expected. "I just wish I could relax with Ian. I can't, and I can't help thinking that it's because we're so different."

"I can't relax with Abernathy, either. But guys are supposed to be different. It would be boring if we were all alike. Actually, I think Ian is terrific. I like talking to Ian better than to Abernathy. When Abernathy and I were alone on the beach, I really found it hard to talk to him."

Abby gave Colette a sideways glance. "Do you think it was wrong of me to let him buy me the shirt?" she asked. "He said that he was really, really sorry for calling me a Jewish Princess, that he didn't mean anything bad by it. He said that at Andover everyone always makes gross jokes to each other. He said that he gets called 'white bread' all the time." The womanly look Colette had glimpsed was gone. Abby looked young again, and so anxious that Colette couldn't stand the thought that Abernathy might hurt her.

"I don't think it was wrong to let him buy you a shirt. He really wanted to. After all, I let Ian buy me a shirt." Colette looked at herself in the dressing-room mirror. "What do you think the kids at school are going to think when they hear that we drove to Maine just so our dates could buy us presents?"

"They're going to think that it's just something a JAP would do," said Abby.

"Hey, cut that out. You're not a JAP. You're not even anything at all like one. So don't put yourself down just to please Abernathy." Colette surprised both herself and Abby by the vehemence in her voice. Abby stared at her.

"I don't put myself down."

"You do sometimes. Ian notices it."

"Well, I'll try to correct myself so that it pleases Ian."

Colette hadn't wanted to hurt Abby, and

now she felt self-conscious. "Come on, Abb, don't get all huffy. Let's put on our shirts."

They both put them on and looked in the mirror. On Abby, the shirt was sexless and boxy. If anything it looked worse on Colette. It made her look fat and dumpy.

Abby reached over and turned the collar up on Colette's shirt. She looked at it critically. "Try tying the ends around your waist," she suggested.

"It's pretty awful, isn't it?" said Colette.

"It's not terrific," said Abby. "But listen, what can you expect from Wasps?"

Colette tried tying the shirt tails tightly. At least it gave her a waist. With the collar turned up it didn't look half bad. Abby did the same to her shirt.

They walked out on the showroom floor and Colette glanced at her watch. "We've got to call our parents," she said. "And we'd better get our stories straight."

"We'll just tell them that the very proper Abernathys have invited us to stay in Manchester. As long as we're together, it'll be okay. If I were by myself, my father would throw a shit-fit. But as long as I'm with you, he always thinks I won't get in trouble."

"Mine, too. Let's find the guys and get to a phone."

They walked through the aisles of the vast store, nearly empty of customers. Colette spotted Ian by a counter.

"Where's Abernathy?" Abby asked.

"He'll be here in a second. You look good in

your shirts, both of you." He looked sly. "In fact, you both look good in purple. . . ."

Abby grinned at him. "Careful, buddy, those are fighting words. So where is Abernathy? Colette and I have to call our parents."

"Here I am." Abernathy appeared behind Abby. He was carrying a big shopping bag.

"What did you get for yourself?" Abby asked.

Abernathy only looked mysterious. "Let's get out of here, and I'll show you."

"You didn't steal anything, did you?" Abby whispered.

Abernathy put his arm around her. "Don't worry. Do you think I could have asked for a shopping bag and then stuck something in it? No, I paid for it. Let's go."

When they were outside, Colette was glad that she had the chamois shirt on. With the sun down the air was cold. She wondered when she should give Ian his earmuffs; somehow it seemed like something that she should give to him when they were alone. She wished now that she had brought her down jacket, or maybe bought earmuffs for herself. Abby was shivering, too. She wrapped her arms around herself.

"You're still cold after we bought the shirt?" Abernathy asked.

Abby nodded. "But forget it. You'll probably tell me you know of a great store in Nova Scotia where they sell handpicked goose-down jackets. Let's just go back. After Co-

lette and I call our parents. I'll feel better
when that's over with."

"Okay, but you might as well be warm."
Abernathy reached into the bag and pulled
out a beautiful down vest. It was navy, lined
with purple, and it had a rainbow on the back
made out of satin.

"I thought this would go with your shirt,"
he said, handing the vest to Abby.

Abby looked shocked. "You bought this for
me? I can't . . . What are you going to tell
your parents? Do you always buy girls presents like this? This is crazy."

Abernathy got angry. "My parents have
nothing to do with this. *I* bought it for you. If
you don't like it I can return it."

Abby held it, tight. "It's beautiful. It's
just . . . I don't know. We don't know kids
who give each other expensive presents. It
was crazy enough just coming up here on a
whim."

"I'm not a 'kid' giving expensive presents,"
snapped Abernathy. Then he looked contrite
again. "Please, Abby, take it. I want you to
have it."

Abby softened. "It's beautiful. I love it."
She put it on. It looked wonderful on her.

Abby reached up and kissed Abernathy
lightly on the lips. Colette felt awkward
watching them kiss in the parking lot of L. L.
Bean. Ian stood with his hands in his pockets.

"I knew you had a vest," he said. "That's
why I didn't get you one."

"Oh, Ian," said Colette quickly. She felt

both embarrassed and sorry for him. She wondered if he always felt that he had to keep up with Abernathy. "Hey," she whispered. "Close your eyes."

"Huh?" Ian shook his head.

"Just close your eyes. Do as I say."

Ian closed his eyes. Colette got the earmuffs out of her purse. She stretched them apart and put them on Ian's ears.

He opened his eyes, and his hands went to his ears. He felt the earmuffs and laughed.

"They're a present," said Colette. "To keep your ears covered."

"And pinned down," said Ian.

Chapter Nine

In the car, Ian took off his earmuffs. He sat forward with his arms on the front seat and plunked the muffs on Abernathy's head.

"Hey, watch it, buddy," snapped Abernathy. "I'm driving." He took the earmuffs off and stared at them as if they were an object he had never seen before. "What the hell are these?"

"They're a present from Colette," said Ian. His voice was loud and high. "Aren't they great?"

"Great," said Abernathy, but he flung them over his shoulder so that they landed on Ian's lap.

"Sorry, I can't hear you. I got earmuffs on my banana." Ian cracked up. He glanced at Colette. "You know that old joke about the man who walks down the street with a banana in his ear and someone asks him why. He says, 'I can't hear you. I got a banana in my ear.'" Ian pointed to the earmuffs on his lap. "Well, I've got earmuffs on my banana. Get it?"

Abby and Abernathy laughed. Colette didn't. She didn't like him making fun of her present.

"I know of a bar near here. You two can make your calls from there," said Abernathy.

"Hey!" said Ian, leaning forward and poking Abby in the arm. "What did one ear say to the other?"

"I don't know," said Abby. "What did one ear say to the other?"

"Meet you around the block."

Abby groaned. "I should get you together with my little sister. She loves bad jokes."

"Why is a bad joke like a worn-down pencil?"

"Because it has no point," said Abby.

Colette wished Ian would stop with the bad jokes. She felt a little sick to her stomach. She was worried about calling and lying to her parents. Ian was acting like a hyperactive kid, bouncing around in the backseat and refusing to talk to her. She was worried that he was mad at her. She was scared about Abernathy driving after dark. She was nervous about going into the bar. This trip was making her nuts!

Finally they pulled into a parking lot. An orange neon sign flashed BAR/PIZZA alternately. The building was made to look like a fake log cabin. There were only a couple of cars in the parking lot.

The bartender gave them a suspicious look as they slid into a booth. "Let's go make our calls," said Colette.

Abby nodded.

Ian stood up. He dug his hands deep into his pockets and came up with a fistful of change. "Here," he said.

"No, thanks," said Colette through clenched teeth.

"Take it," insisted Ian.

Colette shook her head. She wanted to pay for the phone call herself.

Colette knew that the earmuffs had been a bad joke, that Ian thought she was making fun of him. She had just wanted to buy him a present, but she wished now that she had had the money to buy him something nice, not something that made fun of the one thing that embarrassed him. She decided that she had been stupid for buying the earmuffs. It was like Ian buying her a size *D* bra. Why couldn't she have thought more before she did it?

"I'll go to the phone with you," said Abby quickly.

Colette was glad. Maybe she'd have a chance to ask Abby what she should do. A group of men came into the bar as she and Abby went to the phone. They turned to stare.

"They're staring at you in that vest," said Colette.

"Don't be stupid. When men stare at us, it's at you. And you're looking terrific lately, even in that shirt. You look sexy, and it's not just your boobs. Even your face has changed."

Colette stared at her. "You know, that's what I was thinking today. Earlier, in the store, you suddenly looked different. More like a woman."

Abby hugged her. "Maybe it's true what they say about sex."

"What do they say about sex?" asked Colette.

"It makes you sexy."

Colette laughed.

"Look, if a few French kisses do this to us, can you imagine what will happen if we go all the way?" asked Abby.

"I don't feel very sexy right now," said Colette. "I think Ian's mad at me because I bought him the earmuffs. He must think I was making fun of his ears."

"Are you kidding? He was thrilled. He was just as excited as I was about my vest. Oh, Colette, isn't it beautiful? What are my folks gonna say when they see it? They might not like it that he bought me an expensive present. I might have to keep it at your house."

"That's okay," mumbled Colette. Abby didn't seem to think that her problem with Ian was worth talking about. That hurt a little—actually, more than a little.

The phone was in a little alcove in the front of the bar. Colette wished it were more private. She was scared now, frightened that her mother would be able to smell out the lie and ask to speak to Abernathy's parents. She felt as if the entire afternoon had been lived out on a spooky, unreal level. Calling home felt all too real.

Colette dialed her number. The operator told her to deposit $1.75, and the sound of the quarters as they clanked through the machine was loud in Colette's ear. She fumbled, trying to put in the quarters quickly, so that the noise would stop before someone answered.

Her heart sank when she heard her father's voice. She would much rather have spoken to her mother.

She willed her voice to sound normal. "Hi, Dad, it's Colette."

"I recognize the voice. Where are you? You sound like you're in a bar."

Colette swallowed. How could he have guessed so fast? She gave Abby a helpless look. "We're in a sort of restaurant in Manchester. Look, it's so beautiful here, the Abernathys invited Abby and me to stay the night. Is that okay? It'll be really nice here tomorrow. We may go for a little sail. The Abernathys are really nice people."

"Who are the Abernathys? Have I met them?"

"You met their son, James Abernathy. He goes to Andover with my date Ian. Please, Dad, it's really nice here. Abby and I are together. We'll take a train home early tomorrow afternoon."

"Colette, does your mother know about this? She's over at the Y swimming. I don't know how I feel about your spending the night with people we don't know."

"Dad, don't be so old-fashioned. They're a really nice family, and I'm with Abby. It's not as if I'm by myself."

"Well, I guess if it's all right with the Kleins . . . but give me the number where you can be reached."

Colette signaled desperately for Abby.

"Wait a minute, Dad." She put her hand

over the receiver. "He wants their telephone number. What number should I give him?"

"You'd better give him the real one. I'll get it."

"Just a second, Dad. Abby's getting the number."

"Colette, are you sure you're okay? You sound funny." Her father's voice sounded so dripping with concern that it upset Colette. She knew she was being irrational. Her father loved her, and he had a reason to be concerned. She was in a bar up in Maine, lying to him about spending the night in an empty house. But still, Colette felt like he should have trusted her, should have trusted her even as she lied to him.

Abby came back with Abernathy's telephone number written on a napkin that had a picture of a leprechaun drowning in a martini. As Colette read her father the number, she felt like crying. She had to grip the telephone tightly.

"I'll call you in the morning," Colette said quickly. "Give my love to Mom."

"Okay, sweetheart." Her father laughed nervously. "I guess this is what they mean about letting go. I'm supposed to not worry when my daughter decides to turn an afternoon date into an overnight."

"Daddy," said Colette desperately, "I'm just spending the night with Abby and a group of friends. I haven't gone off anywhere." Colette wondered as she piled lie upon lie if she'd ever straighten things out with her father. Would she ever tell the truth? "I've got to go."

"I know," said her father, sounding hurt. "Have a good time, sweetheart."

Colette hung up the phone, feeling drained.

"You look terrible all of a sudden," said Abby. "Don't think about it. We're not doing anything so wrong."

Colette envied Abby as she eavesdropped on her conversation with her mother. Abby's voice sounded natural and exuberant as she lied about the Abernathys and the wonderful things they had planned for the next morning. She made the Abernathys sound like real people.

Abby hung up the phone. "Well, that's taken care of. We can stop worrying." Colette could think of hundreds and hundreds of things that they could still worry about, such as whether she and Ian would get a chance to talk alone, and what would happen when they got back to Manchester.

"Col, when we get back to Manchester, what do you think's gonna happen?"

"I don't know," said Colette, relieved that Abby had brought it up. "That's exactly what I was wondering. What do you think?"

"Well, if you don't mind. I'm sort of scared to be left alone with Abernathy. I mean, for the whole night. It all feels so rushed. I'm not ready to sleep with him."

"I'm not ready, either," said Colette, feeling extremely relieved. She hadn't even realized how uptight the question of sleeping arrangements had been making her. "Oh, Abb, let's stick together."

"Together!" whispered Abby. She stuck out her hand. Colette shook it. Whatever happened, at least she knew that she and Abby would be together.

When they got back to Ian and Abernathy, the bartender was standing over their table, scowling at a small piece of paper in his hand. He was a tall, skinny, balding man with a knobby forehead. He wore glasses, and he looked tired.

"Do you girls have I.D., too?" he asked.

Colette and Abby glanced at each other.

"You don't look a day over seventeen," the bartender said, looking straight at Colette. Colette felt flattered. He thought she was two years older than she was. "I want you all to leave."

"Wait a minute," said Abernathy. "All we want is a beer; the girls don't want anything. Aren't we entitled to date younger chicks?"

The bartender twisted his lips. He stared at Abby. "She looks like she's still jailbait. Get out of here, all of you."

Abernathy crossed his arms in front of his chest. "We've got a constitutional right," he said.

The bartender shoved his face within inches of Abernathy's nose. "You want me to call the cops and have them check your I.D., buddy?"

"I want my beer," Abernathy said petulantly.

A couple of customers who had just come in were now staring at them. Colette realized that except for a waitress standing in the corner, she and Abby were the only females in the place. The waitress was old, in her forties, and she looked very bored. Colette remembered reading about several gang rapes of girls in bars, and suddenly she was scared.

"Let's go," Colette said quickly. But Abernathy grabbed Abby's wrist.

"No, my date will stay with me while this gentleman serves me my beer."

Abby pulled away. "I agree with Colette, I think we should go," she whispered. Abernathy's grip tightened. The bartender looked at him with disgust. "Don't get cute."

Colette pulled on Ian's arm. "He's being an asshole," she whispered. "Please, let's go."

Ian shook her off angrily. He sat down next to Abernathy. Abernathy smiled at him, a conspirator's smile. They thought they were so cute with their fake I.D.s Colette was furious. She hoped the bartender would throw them out.

"We don't want trouble," said Ian in his most affected boarding-school voice. "Why don't you just get my friend his beer, and one for me, too, and we'll be on our way. We're not asking you to serve the girls."

The overbred niceness in his voice infuriated the bartender. It was obvious that neither he nor Abernathy was twenty-one, Maine's drinking age. They seemed to be implying that their class and upbringing demanded that the bartender serve them, regardless of the law.

Colette hated the arrogance in their tone.

"I'm leaving," she said.

"No, you're not," said Ian. He grabbed her with the identical gesture that Abernathy had used on Abby. Colette snapped her arm back without realizing the force she was using, and she ended up elbowing the bartender in the stomach.

She turned to apologize and heard, but didn't see, Abernathy's loud laugh.

"That's it!" shouted the bartender. "You fucking kids get out of here or I'll call the cops!"

"It was an accident," cried Colette. "I didn't hit you on purpose. I was feeling sorry for you."

"Look, you college kids get out of here."

Abernathy laughed, and Ian laughed with him. Obviously they were thrilled to be mistaken for college kids, but Colette was scared.

"Let's go," she said.

Ian and Abernathy shook their heads. "Our I.D. is good," said Ian. "You have to serve us."

"I don't have to do anything," said the bartender. He reached across the table and grabbed Ian by his jacket. He was about a foot taller than Ian and had him standing on his tiptoes. Ian pushed the bartender.

The man stumbled. He drew his hand back and Colette yelled. She was sure he was going to hit Ian. Her scream surprised the bartender. He glanced at her, and when he wasn't looking, Abernathy stood up and shoved the table into his stomach.

The bartender stumbled back, and his hand hit Colette in the breast. "Ouch!" cried Colette.

"Don't you touch her," said Ian.

"It was an accident," said Colette.

"You kids have thirty seconds to get out of here," snarled the bartender.

Ian and Abernathy looked at each other. Colette realized that they were enjoying themselves. If they were at all scared, they didn't show it. They crossed their arms in front of their chests.

The bartender grabbed Ian again and tried to force him out. Ian fought back. Two of the other customers joined in, and it took them much less than thirty seconds to shove Abernathy and Ian out the door.

Colette and Abby followed them. As she walked out of the bar, Colette was furious. She hated Ian at that moment.

Outside in the parking lot, Ian and Abernathy were laughing, their arms around each other.

"You guys were assholes, you know that!" yelled Colette.

Ian looked up. Colette's voice was loud. Two couples had just driven up to the bar, and they turned to stare at her.

"Hey, Colette, quiet down," warned Ian.

"Oh, are you afraid of a scene?" she yelled. "What do you think you just had in that bar? That was a scene, but that was cute, because you guys had your fake I.D.'s and your fake upper-class accents."

"What do our accents have to do with anything?"

"Why don't you just get my friend his beer, and one for me, too, and we'll be on our way!" yelled Colette, mimicking the way Ian had sounded. "You had no right to ask him to serve you. You're underage. And Abernathy has to drive. Do you know how many kids get killed 'cause they're drunk when they're driving?"

"Ah, stop sounding as if you're practicing for a role in *Little House on the Prairie,* will you?" said Abernathy. "You always sound like you're seeing yourself in a movie."

Abernathy's words hit hard. She wondered how Abernathy knew that she often did see herself as if with a third eye, even now when she was acting like a screaming witch.

"And you always see yourself as Mr. Super-cool, don't you? Well, you and your friend can go back to Andover. I'm not going another mile with you. You can take Manchester and your big house and shove it. Do you hear me?"

"I think everyone inside the bar must be hearing you," said Ian. "Let's get in the car."

"Colette, calm down," said Abby. "He's right. You're making a scene." Colette glanced at Abby. She looked frightened. But Colette stubbornly planted her feet. She wouldn't move.

"I'm not going," she said.

"Colette," said Ian, as if he were talking to a child. "Get in the car."

His voice sounded so reasonable that Colette felt like screaming louder. "I'm not going in his fucking car. I'm gonna take a bus home."

"Colette, stop it," said Ian. "I'm sorry you're upset, but let's go."

"Do you have ears . . . or do they stick out so far that you can't hear?" Colette bit her lip. She couldn't believe that she had said anything that mean. She felt as if she had gone too far. "I'm not going with you," she said more quietly. She meant it. She would take a bus home somehow and get to her own bed and pull the covers up over her head. And she might never come out.

Chapter Ten

"I don't know where you get the bus," said Abernathy in a clipped voice.

"Just drop me off at a gas station," said Colette as they got into the car. "I'll hitchhike to the nearest place the bus stops." Had she really just said that? Every muscle in her body felt tight.

"I'm going to go with her," said Abby. Her voice sounded shaky.

"You don't have to," said Colette. She wished that there was some way that she could make the last five minutes disappear. Ian had stopped talking to her. He sat with his arms crossed, looking rigid.

Colette was in the front seat with Abby. Ian sat alone in the back. "Are you okay?" whispered Abby.

Colette nodded. She wasn't, but she didn't trust herself to speak. They drove down Route 1. Ian was silent in the backseat. Was it just going to end on such a crazy note? Why couldn't he just say "I'm sorry"? Why couldn't she?

She saw the lights of an Exxon station up ahead.

"Pull in there, please," Colette said. She stole a glance into the backseat. Ian was huddled in a corner, staring out the window.

Colette wished he would say something, anything to break the silence.

Abernathy stopped the car. "You're crazy," he said.

Colette stepped out. The night air seemed even colder than before. "I'll find out where we get the bus," she said.

"Colette," said Abernathy. "Cut it out. Enough is enough. You've made your point. Come on back in the car, and let's go."

"I'm not doing this to make a point. I want to take a bus." Colette thought she sounded like she was ten years old. "Besides, I never understood what 'enough is enough' means."

"You know, you're a real pill," said Abernathy.

"I know. Just drive off. I won't ever bother you again."

"Ian," said Abernathy. "Talk to her."

Ian shook his head.

"Let's go," said Colette.

The sodium lights from the gas station gave off an eerie yellow glow. The gas station attendant looked up when he saw them.

"The key for the ladies' room is on the pegboard inside. It's around the corner."

"No—we need to know where we can get the next bus to Boston," said Colette. "Does it stop around here?"

The gas station attendant looked like he was about eighteen. He had a line of pimples down each cheek. "You can't get there from here."

"Is that supposed to be a joke?" Abby asked.

The guy gave a high-pitched giggling laugh. "Sure, it's the line that all tourists want us to give. You know, it's the story about a tourist who stops a Maine farmer for directions how to get somewhere. And the punch line is, 'Come to think of it, you can't get there from here.'"

"Very funny," said Abby. "But would you please answer our question?"

"I did answer it. You can't get there from here. The bus goes along the expressway. But I get off in just a few minutes. If you girls want, I'll drive you to the expressway and to the bus stop." The gas station attendant looked over at the car. Ian and Abernathy had gotten out and were glaring at them. "Had a little trouble with your dates, did you?" asked the attendant.

Colette nodded. Abby grabbed her arm. "Let's talk about this a minute. Colette, this is nuts. We can't go with him."

Abernathy yelled to them. "Come on," he said. "You've done your grandstand play, now let's go."

"Shut up," said Abby.

Colette felt ready to burst into tears. "I'm sorry, Abby. I just feel—I don't know—Ian hates me now. I'd rather die than drive back with them. I just want to be home!"

"Okay. I admit they acted stupid in the bar, but it's not that big a deal. This isn't like you."

"I know." Colette sniffled. "It's not a question of forgiveness. But I just can't drive with them anymore. Ian hates me. I could see it in his eyes when I started screaming. Maybe I am going nuts. Crack-up in a gas station in Maine! What a title."

"Yeah, we can write a song about it, but meanwhile I'm a little scared of this gas station guy."

"It's okay." Colette sniffed. "You go with Ian and Abernathy. I'll be fine."

"Now I know you're nuts." Abby shook her head. "I'm not going to leave you alone with that pimply creep. We're in this together. If you want to leave them, I'll go along with you."

"You'd do that for me, even if it meant losing Abernathy? He's really mad at me, you know."

"I'm gonna go talk to them," said Abby. "Wait here for me."

Colette hunched down on the curb that separated the gas station from a field half-filled with old wrecks of cars. It looked very desolate. Colette decided that she had never been more miserable in her life. Yet part of her knew that most of the melodrama was something she was creating. She felt like she was looking through a window and watching herself act out a scene. It didn't seem real.

The gas station attendant came over to her. "Are you having a bad trip?" he asked.

"The worst," agreed Colette.

"What're you on?"

"Not that kind of a bad trip," said Colette quickly. He smiled down at her.

Colette stood up. She had to stifle a desire to laugh. It all seemed so ridiculous and melodramatic. *A bad trip!* Boy, was she having a *bad* trip! She wished that she could share the joke with Ian. Abby was walking toward her, her head down, looking defeated. Colette glanced at Abernathy's car. He was in the driver's seat. She tried to see if Ian had moved to the front seat.

Colette looked up as she saw the headlights of Abernathy's car go on. She couldn't leave Abby and herself stranded out here in the middle of nowhere. "Wait!" she yelled. She ran toward the car. The headlights blinded her.

"Hey, wait!" she screamed.

The car stopped. Ian got out and ran to her. "Colette, please."

"I'm sorry—" Colette started to say.

"We weren't leaving," said Ian. "Abernathy was just going to turn the car around."

"I scared myself. I'm sorry. I'm sorry."

Ian held her. "I just don't understand what is happening."

"Neither do I," said Colette. "I just got so mad at you that I didn't know what to do."

Abby came up to them. "Colette?"

"I'm sorry, Abb." Colette was blubbering. She tried to sniff back the tears. "Oh, Abb, please forgive me. I didn't mean to make a scene."

"You scared the shit out of me," said Abby.

"Me, too," said Ian.

"Me, three," said Colette. "I just got so mad, I couldn't control myself."

"You're telling us," said Abby. "I had visions of us going off in the night with that gas station guy and never getting home."

Abernathy walked over to them. "Would someone mind filling me in on the next act of this melodrama?"

"It's the end of the act," said Colette. "I'm sorry. I didn't mean to throw such a fit."

"So, you'll get back in the car?" asked Abernathy. "We can go home?"

Colette nodded, feeling deflated. She looked up and saw the gas station attendant staring at them. Colette walked over to him. "I'm sorry, but thanks, anyway. My friend and I decided to let our dates drive us home, after all."

Colette felt oddly flattered that the gas station attendant liked her. She walked back to the car, swinging her hips just a little as she walked.

Abby was in the front seat next to Abernathy. Nobody said anything for several minutes. Colette felt as if she had created a dangerous aura around herself. She had proved to be unpredictable, a surprise even to herself. She wondered what Ian was thinking.

"Is it all right with everybody if I put on the radio?" Abernathy asked. He turned up the volume, effectively isolating Colette and Ian in the backseat.

In the front Abby was sitting close to Abernathy. They were deep in what looked like a relaxed and easy conversation. Then Abby put her head on Abernathy's lap.

Colette felt exhausted. She leaned back

against the car seat. Ian continued to stare out the window.

Finally, he spoke. "I couldn't take it when you started screaming," he said in a low voice. Colette looked over at him. He still wasn't looking at her. "I just couldn't stand it."

"I was mad," said Colette.

"I know." Ian turned his head. "You made that very clear."

"You're still mad at *me*."

"No, I mean, you were probably right to be mad at us for trying to get the guy to serve us, but when you started screaming in public, I hated it. I really did."

In some ways Colette thought she had been magnificent when she had finally let go and screamed that they were assholes. "Well, if you don't want me to express my feelings, I don't know. I said I was sorry for causing such a scene. What more can I say?"

"How come you're the only one who gets to express herself? I'm sorry if I didn't appreciate the little act you pulled at the gas station. It just wasn't my style."

"I'm sure. I'm sure it was too Jewish—too ethnic for your white-bread taste." Colette couldn't believe they were fighting again. It seemed as if both of them just blurted out things that hurt, or, to be fair, it seemed like she was incapable of controlling herself with Ian. Either way, it was clear now that they were mismatched.

"Who cares about that crap? You're not going to bring up that shit again about being

Jewish and my *not* being Jewish. I never think about that stuff."

"I don't believe you!"

"I don't lie. And I don't need you to tell me I'm lying. I don't *need* you at all." Ian crossed his arms over his chest.

Colette stared out at the night, watching the reflectors on the side of the road, trying to count them as they went by. Anything to keep her mind a blank.

It all seemed horribly ironic. Abby was in the front seat, talking intimately with Abernathy. And now she and Ian had broken up! She wasn't even going to get a chance to reject him; he was rejecting her.

She felt Ian's hand on her arm. She pulled away, hugging herself tighter. "Colette, please . . . talk to me."

"Don't worry, I'm not going to make another scene. Now please stay on your side of the seat."

Abby turned around. "Are you okay back there?"

"Never better," said Ian sarcastically.

Colette felt miserable. Her hand was on the door handle, and she pictured herself pulling it and tumbling out onto the road. Then he'd feel sorry.

Colette closed her eyes. She felt tears coming. It was all such a mess. Even Abby was growing away from her, and it was all her fault. Her fault for getting so angry, her fault for introducing Abby to Abernathy. She leaned her head against the window. The glass was cold. She looked out and she could see the waning moon.

Never had she felt so lonely.

She glanced over at Ian. He was staring out the window in an almost identical position. They could be bookends. He turned and caught her staring at him. He smiled at her, a tentative smile, but one that seemed to plead with her. Then he did something totally unexpected. He blew her a kiss.

Colette felt the skin around the edges of her eyes relax. She smiled back. Ian inched over from the window. He drew an imaginary line on the seat.

"See," he whispered. "I'm still on my side, but I'm going to blow kisses at you. There's no rule against blowing kisses. I'm not violating your space."

He started blowing kisses in her direction. It was so silly. It felt like a game children would play. He looked just like a little boy, holding his hand up to his lips and then sending a kiss in her direction.

Slowly, Colette brought her hand up to her mouth. She blew a kiss over to Ian. Ian reached over and took her hand. He turned it over and began gently tickling her palm.

"My great-aunt used to do this to me when I was little. I always loved it."

"It feels good," Colette said. Ian's fingers circled the fleshy part of her palm. His touch gave her a tender feeling of being cared for.

"What's your great-aunt like?" She was curious about a woman who would so openly touch a child where it felt so good to be touched.

"She was wonderful. She died last year when she was ninety-one. She lived in New York in an apartment near us on Park Avenue. It was decorated all in red and black. She was very proper, but she liked me a lot. I could always tell. I liked her, too."

"I'm sorry she's dead."

"Well, ninety-one is pretty old. And she didn't get senile at all. She loved to party. When I was about thirteen, she taught me to tend bar at her parties, and she'd pay me for it. I was pretty good. Some of my mom's friends ask me to tend bar now. On New Year's Eve last year I made fifty dollars. It's fun. When I applied to boarding schools, they asked me what were my hobbies, and did I sometimes do jobs that earned me money? You should have seen some of the admission people's faces when I told them I was a part-time bartender."

Colette listened. His voice sounded so soothing. She liked hearing him talk about his great-aunt and being a bartender, but it seemed so weird. They were still in the middle of a horrible fight. How could they be sitting next to each other, talking so calmly, when they hadn't resolved anything?

"What about our fight?" she asked. "Aren't we going to talk about it?"

"Do we have to?"

Colette nodded. But she picked up his hand and began tickling his palm. She didn't know why she did that, but she was scared of changing the mood again.

"That feels good," Ian said. "I'm sorry about the fight in the bar. It all happened so damned fast."

"It wasn't the fight in the bar that got me angry, but the way that you and Abernathy acted—as if the bartender *had* to serve you. You had fake I.D.s. He did have a right to throw you out."

"Colette, are we going to have to go through every word of it again? You've already told me I was an asshole. I agreed. You were an asshole to make such a scene, so we're even. All I can tell you is that even when you were right, I couldn't stand it when you were screaming at me in the parking lot. I guess I just don't like scenes. It bothered me. I didn't know what to do. You really seemed out of control."

"I felt out of control."

Ian was silent. Colette didn't know what to say, either. She wanted him to say that nothing about her bothered him, that he thought she was perfect just the way she was.

Chapter Eleven

Finally, they arrived back in Manchester. Abby had fallen asleep in the front seat. Abernathy woke her up. Her face was red and creased. Colette felt so tired that all she cared about was lying down, but nobody had said anything about going to sleep and who would sleep where.

They stumbled into Abernathy's house. Ian stretched. "I have a feeling that this was one of those days that's going to be better to talk about than it was to go through."

"I was thinking that, too," said Colette.

She looked at her watch. It was only eleven o'clock, but it felt like three in the morning. Abby seemed so tired she looked almost drugged. She flopped onto the couch face-down. Abernathy looked at her. "There she is, my little rock star. I thought you two were such high-energy types that nothing could tire you out."

Colette sat down on the edge of the couch. Abby lifted her head and winked at her. "Where can Abby and I sleep?" Colette asked.

"If I said 'with me' would I get into trouble?" Abernathy asked.

Colette shook her head. "Sorry, Charlie, come on, just point us to a bed."

"Wait, how about a good-night beer," said Abernathy. He got one for himself and Ian and handed one to Colette. "Come on, it won't kill you."

"Okay," said Colette. She took the beer. She realized as she sipped it how glad she was to be out of the car. Abby sat up sleepily. "I really am zonked."

"Come on, I'll show you where you can sleep." Abernathy helped her up. "Don't worry, Colette, I'm not going to take advantage of her fatigued state."

"Why not?" Abby asked. "How come nobody ever wants to take advantage of me?"

Ian laughed. "Don't worry. Hey, Abernathy, no fooling. She's dead tired, let her be."

"Abby, did you know that Ian has declared himself your protector?" said Abernathy.

Abby lurched over to Ian. She kissed him good night on the top of the head, as if she were kissing an uncle.

Abruptly, Abby turned around and sat back down on the couch next to Colette. "We made a pact."

Colette took a sip of her beer. "To our pact." Colette toasted Abby with the beer can and then gave her a sip.

"What's the pact?" Abernathy asked.

Abby put her finger to her lips. "It's a secret."

Abernathy held a hand out to Abby and helped her off the couch. She giggled happily. "I'm all right. I have my magic vest on." She twirled around, opening the snaps of her vest, but she tripped and fell toward Abernathy.

Colette watched them walk out of the room. She felt nervous now that she was actually alone with Ian. It felt strange to be alone in a house with just the four of them.

Ian hauled himself out of the easy chair. He came and sat down on the couch next to Colette. "You know, you are a worrywart," he said softly.

"How can you tell?"

"It shows on your face. Everything you feel shows up on your face. It's amazing." He kissed her and tried to force her teeth apart with his tongue. He moved his hands up and down over the chamois shirt. Then he moved his lips up to her ear and covered it with his mouth, flicking his tongue inside it.

His hands came around to the front of her shirt, and he tried to unbutton the middle button. Colette tried to stop him.

"Don't," she whispered. "Please."

Ian stopped. He pulled back. "Why not? What's wrong?"

"I think I should go up to Abby," Colette said stubbornly.

Ian dropped his hands to his side. "What are you going to do if she and Abernathy are making out? Leave them alone!"

"You and Abernathy plotted this all out, didn't you? Very clever."

"Oh, sure . . . it was all a diabolical plot. We were going to lure you up here. Jesus, Colette, sometimes I think you see the whole world as if it were a bad movie. All I wanted to do was hold you and kiss you. You feel so good."

Colette felt hurt. "Do you really think I see things like a bad movie?"

"A little." Ian's voice was teasing.

"Well, this is all new for me. For Abby, too. We're both a little scared."

"Am I that scary?" Ian's fingers traced her cheekbones and tickled her ears.

Colette shook her head. "Sort of. You're sort of that scary. Ian, I'm so tired. All I want to do is find Abby and go to sleep. Please."

Ian spread his hands apart. "I'm not stopping you."

"Ian, don't be mad at me."

"Who's mad at you?" His voice was tight.

Abernathy came into the room. "Abby's calling for you," he said. Colette thought he sounded disgusted. "It's the second room on the left. There are two beds in there."

Colette gave Ian a last glance. She felt torn between a desire to stay and be with him and a wish to be with Abby, where it was safe.

Colette opened the door. Abby was lying on one of the two twin beds in the room. The covers were pulled up to her chin, and she looked very young.

Colette sat down on the other bed. The room was painted pale blue, and the headboards of the twin beds were white with cornflowers painted on them. It was obviously a "girl's" room. Colette wondered who it belonged to.

"Abby, are you asleep?" Colette asked.

Abby opened her eyes. Colette saw that she had been crying. "Abb, what's wrong?"

Abby sat up in bed and brought her knees

to her chest. She wiped her eyes with the back of her hand. Colette put her arms around her. She hadn't seen Abby cry in years.

"Abb?"

"I blew it," sniffed Abby. "Blew it, 'cause I'm such a prude."

"What did you blow?" Colette asked softly.

Abby looked up at her and gave a half-smile through her tears. "Actually, you just made a dirty joke."

"What's the matter? No jokes. Something's really got you upset?"

Abby just shook her head. "I shouldn't have been such a 'fraidy-cat. That's what he called me. It's what you call a ten-year-old."

"Why did he call you that?"

Abby didn't answer. "Hand me my vest, will you?"

Colette got up and gave Abby the vest Abernathy had bought her. It had been tossed onto a rose-colored easy chair in the corner.

Abby stroked it as if it were a pet. "It's beautiful, isn't it?"

Colette nodded.

Abby looked so pitiful that Colette could hardly stand it.

"Did you and Abernathy have a fight?" she asked.

"We sort of did."

"What happened?"

"Well, when he was driving—you know, when we had the music on loud? I put my head on his lap, and he wanted me to—stroke him—down there. I was scared to, so I pretended to fall asleep. But then when he brought me up here, he made a joke that he knew I was faking being asleep. That's when he called me a 'fraidy-cat. I would rather have had him call me a cockteaser. At least that's more grown-up."

"Only you could make a joke right now. Come on, Abb. He doesn't have a right to call you names."

"But he bought me the present. He invited me out here. He's not a kid. He's seventeen. He wasn't asking so much. But I got scared. I've never touched anyone down there."

"Me neither. But I don't think you should feel bad about it. You've got a right to take these things slowly."

"Well, you can say that because Ian's not gonna run away. But I could lose Abernathy. He just looked like he didn't even care anymore. Why should he? I *am* a 'fraidy-cat. A short, flat-chested, Jewish 'fraidy-cat."

"Abb, stop that! You're terrific. You're funny. You're great company. And shit, Abernathy doesn't have a right to make you do something you're scared of. Besides, think of it this way. You might have saved all our lives. I sure wouldn't have wanted Abernathy driving while you were, you know . . ."

"That's me," said Abby. "Little Miss Safe Driving."

"Abb, stop putting yourself down," said Colette.

Abby turned on her. "That's getting to be quite a refrain you've got. Let me tell you, it makes me feel just terrific to think about you and Ian talking about me. And who are you to lecture me? You and Ian don't get any awards for couple of the year, you know. I don't think that crazy little scene about 'I'm taking the bus' won you any Miss Sane Teenager Award."

Colette stared at Abby, feeling as if she had been struck. Abby had never talked to her that way. They never fought or argued.

Colette lay down on the other bed. "I'm sorry," she said automatically.

"Let's just go to sleep," said Abby. "We're probably both tired. Good night."

Colette turned out the light and lay in the dark. For the first time that she could remember, it didn't feel easy being in a room alone with Abby. She curled into a ball on her side. She thought she heard a telephone ringing downstairs. The last thing she remembered before falling asleep was worrying that it was her father calling.

Chapter Twelve

When Colette woke up, the sun was streaming in the windows. Abby was dressed and looking out the window. She came and sat down on Colette's bed.

"You can see the ocean from here," said Abby. She picked up the edge of Colette's bedspread and played with it. "I'm sorry about what I said last night. I must have just been tired and upset. I'm sorry."

"Oh, Abby, I'm sorry, too. I couldn't stand fighting with you. Look, no guy is worth it if we start feeling creepy with each other."

"It wasn't your fault. It was mine."

"No," argued Colette. "It was my fault. Ian's right. I get on my high horse, and I act like little Miss Know-it-All. It's disgusting."

"Stop putting yourself down," said Abby with a teasing note in her voice, but she sounded wistful.

Colette laughed. "Touché. Anyhow, it was a night to remember."

"Yeah, our big night." Abby sighed. "We spend the night with two guys and here we are—together at last."

Colette didn't care. She felt such relief that she and Abby were still friends.

"I wonder whether Abernathy and I are doomed?" Abby got up and looked out the window. She was acting so much like a tragic heroine that Colette had to laugh.

"Doomed?"

"Maybe I'm just not the kind of a girl that guys will ever feel passionately about."

Colette heard Abby putting herself down again, but she was scared to tell her. Instead she said, "I don't think Abernathy's a really passionate kind of guy," she said tentatively. "He likes to act cool. It would be hard to find out what he's really feeling."

"But that's just what he shows on the outside," said Abby. "On the inside, he's different."

Abby picked up her vest, which was lying on the floor near the bed. "I'm gonna go looking for him and wake him up," she said. "It's a brand-new day. I'm going to tell him I'm sorry."

"Sorry for what? He's the one who should say he's sorry."

"Oh, Colette, don't be such a prude. Besides, maybe we both can be sorry. Everything isn't always black and white."

Colette heard echoes of herself with Ian, always saying "I'm sorry." She knew that Abby didn't have anything to be sorry about.

"Do you want to go wake up Ian?"

Colette didn't know what she wanted to do. In many ways her first choice would be to be back in Cambridge, at home in her own bed.

"I don't know. We didn't actually part last night on the best of terms."

"I don't understand you. Ian's really sweet."

"I know, but—"

"But what?"

"It all just seems so complicated. They're such high-class Wasps."

"Colette, I think you have gone a little nuts about this. You never used to care whether anyone was Jewish or not."

"It's not that he's not Jewish. It's that he's so Waspy."

"I think you're just looking for something to hold against Ian." Abby laughed. "Our first adventure with guys and what happens? You and I sleep together, the way we've been sleeping together all our lives. Our parents would never believe us—" Abby stopped.

Colette looked as if she were about to cry.

"Hey, is something really wrong?" asked Abby. I was joking. Come on, despite everything that happened, it was sort of fun, wasn't it? I think you're too tough on Ian. He really cares for you. Ian's great. He's like an older brother I never had. Let's stop making such a big deal about everything and go wake them up. We can sing them that old Everly Brothers song, 'Wake Up, Little Susie.'"

Colette got out of bed. She felt grubby and still tired. "Are you sure this is an adventure?" she asked.

They walked out into the hall. There were at least six different doors, and Abernathy and Ian could be behind any of them.

"This house is huge," said Colette. "It's probably got three dozen bedrooms."

"You take that side, I'll take this," said

Abby. She went down to the end of the hall. Colette opened the door closest to her. She expected it to be empty, but Ian was there, in the middle of a big double bed. He was asleep, lying on his side, his hand half off the bed. The covers had slipped halfway off, and his chest was bare.

Colette held her breath. He looked sweet in his sleep. She had a desire to kiss him awake. She tiptoed over to the bed. Just as she was about to bend over him, his hand wrapped around her waist and pulled her down on the bed.

"You were awake," she cried, half-pulling away, but she ended up beside him, on top of the covers.

Ian wrapped his arms around her, holding her tight. His body felt warm and toasty. Colette smiled at him. She loved the feel of the skin of his chest. He kissed her lightly on the lips and then on her ears and her nose. "Good morning, good morning," he said with each kiss. Colette giggled, and Ian kissed her neck.

Colette rolled over so that she was half on top of him. She arched her back and looked at him. "Want to know a secret?" she asked.

Ian nodded his head. He looked eager.

"Can you keep it?" Colette asked. "Promise not to tell Abernathy or anyone?"

Ian took his finger and drew it across her breast, making a cross. "Cross my heart and hope to die."

"That's my heart, dummy."

"No, that's where *my* heart is. See, you

stole my heart, and now it's in there."
With his finger, Ian drew a heart on her
chest.

Colette groaned. "That's so romantic it's
disgusting."

"Well, you asked me to cross my heart, and
that's the only way I could do it. Now that
I've crossed it and hoped to die and everything, tell me this secret."

"I've never been in bed with a guy before.
That's my secret."

"Okay, now you cross my heart . . . and I'll
tell you a secret."

Colette dragged her finger across his chest.
It was smooth, except for a few brown hairs
that circled his nipples. They looked strange
there, as if they didn't belong. Colette liked
the feel of lying on top of him, his arms
crossed over her back, making her feel encir-
cled.

"What's your secret?" she asked.

"I think I love you."

Colette kept studying his chest, not looking up. She drew her finger in circles around
his chest. "I don't think you should say that,"
she said softly. "We have all these weird
fights. We've only known each other a short
time, and it seems like every half hour we
have a fight. Until I met you I never fought
with anyone. Now even Abby and I had sort
of a fight last night."

"What did you fight about?"

"Never mind. It wasn't important, and it
was okay this morning."

Ian kissed her. "Our fights scare me. I

never know when to expect them. They come out of left field."

"So how can you love somebody if you fight all the time?"

"Practice?"

Colette looked up. Ian was looking at her with such a sweet look on his face. He looked gentle. She could see how easily she could hurt him, did hurt him when she lashed out at him. Yet he claimed he loved her. She couldn't say the words back. She lay her head on his chest, and he stroked her hair.

It felt good to lie with him like this. It felt natural, in a way that she had never felt with anyone except Abby.

He kissed her again. This time Colette rolled off his chest. They lay side by side. Ian began to unbutton the purple chamois shirt.

"It's too warm for a shirt like that," he said. "See, it was a diabolical plot after all. I lured you up to Maine so I could buy you a shirt that would make you too hot. . . ."

Ian tried to give an imitation diabolical laugh.

"Very funny." But Colette let him unbutton the top two buttons. He put his hand under her shirt and rested it on top of her bra as if he didn't know what to do next. His fingers curled around the edges of her bra.

Just then there was a knock on the door. Ian groaned. "Shit . . ."

"Colette . . ." whispered Abby. "It's me. . . ."

"Great," said Ian.

Colette sat up in the bed. "Can I let her in?" she asked.

Ian pulled the covers over his chest. "Oh, sure, nothing going on here that can't be interrupted. Just promise me we get to go on where we stopped."

"Don't be a nerd. . . ."

Colette went to the door. Ian waved at Abby.

"Whoops," said Abby as she saw Ian in bed. "I don't think this was the right moment."

"Is anything wrong?" Colette asked.

"Well, I can't find Abernathy. I looked all around. Maybe there's some hidden bedrooms." She looked petulant. "It's not very romantic to have him just disappear into thin air."

"I wouldn't expect too much romance from Abernathy in the morning. It's not his best time," Ian said, but his voice sounded strange. Colette wondered if he was really mad that Abby had interrupted them.

Abby sat down on the edge of the bed. She looked lonely. "I'll leave you two alone," she said. "I think I'll go take a walk on the beach."

Colette glanced at Ian.

"We'll go, too," he said. "I'll show you two something special about this beach."

Colette felt grateful to him for realizing that she didn't want to leave Abby alone. He really could be a wonderful person.

Outside, the sun was so bright that it seemed to etch every tree and rock with a bold outline. From the cliff they could look down at the sea. The water was a bluish-green color. It looked cold. A sailboat was just leaving the harbor. They walked down the rickety staircase. They had to climb over some rocks to get to the beach. It was low tide, and the rocks were slippery with seaweed and barnacles.

The beach was crescent-shaped, with a small rocky island rising in the middle of the bay. The lone sailboat moved past the island, cutting swiftly through the water.

"Take off your shoes," said Ian.

"Why? The water's freezing," said Abby. "I touched it with my hand. It feels like ice."

"Just do as I say," said Ian. Abby cheerfully sat down on the sand and pulled off her Nikes.

"You, too, Colette."

"I don't have to."

"I know, but do it. I want to show you something."

"Come on, Colette," said Abby. "Stop being so suspicious. Take off your shoes."

Colette took off her shoes. "Your socks, too," said Ian.

"Is this some version of strip poker?" asked Colette.

"No. Take off your socks."

Colette and Abby took off their socks.

"Okay, now follow me." Ian jumped up and ran down the beach. Colette and Abby took after him. The sand was soft, which made it hard to run. Their feet made a strange squeaking sound as they ran. Abby could run faster than Colette, and she bolted ahead, matching Ian stride for stride. The beach was about half a mile long. Ian ran to the end of the crescent. He leaned against a rock, catching his breath. Abby climbed up on a rock and stood over him. Ian took a bunch of seaweed and flung it at her.

Colette still had a hundred yards to reach them. They were both laughing. "Go, Colette, go!" shouted Abby as if she were in a race. Colette pumped her arms. The sound of the squeaking sand grew more intense as she ran harder. Ian held his hands out to her and caught her as she made it to the end.

Colette took several deep breaths. Her lungs were bursting.

"Well, did you hear it?" Ian asked.

"Hear what?"

"The singing sand. This beach is called Singing Beach because the sand makes that sound when you run on it."

"I heard it," said Abby. "It was neat."

"For that, we had to run all the way down here?" said Colette, still trying to catch her breath.

"Well, the exercise is good for you," said Ian. He helped Abby down off the rock.

"That was fun," said Abby. "I wonder if Abernathy's up yet."

"Uhhh . . . I don't think so. Well . . ." Ian looked very uncomfortable.

"Well, we'll just have to wake him up. You never told me where he was hidden."

"Abby, he's not here," said Ian. "See that sailboat?" Ian pointed to the huge sailboat just about to disappear behind the island.

"He's out there?" asked Abby. "But why didn't he wait for me to get up? I would have gone with him."

Ian looked more and more uncomfortable. "Well, see, it's not his boat. Someone called last night and asked if he wanted to go, and it's a good friend. And he said yes." Ian's voice trailed off.

"Well, when's he coming back?" asked Abby. "Is he planning on coming back soon?"

Ian dragged his toes through the sand. He looked young. "Uh . . . he'll probably be out there all day. He said to say that he was sorry. He left a train schedule for you."

Abby grabbed her shoes and ran up the stairs. Colette hurried after her, and Ian followed.

Colette found Abby in the room they had shared, lying facedown on the bed, crying. "Abby?" she said quietly, sitting down on the bed next to her.

Abby didn't say anything. Colette picked up the vest. "Come on," said Colette. "Please, Abb, don't cry."

"It's all my fault," sobbed Abby. "If I hadn't been such a prude. He was mad at me, and now I don't even get to say, 'I'm sorry.'" Abby sat up. "Oh, shit. I don't know what to do. I guess I can't wait around here all day until he comes back so I can talk to him."

"I don't think that's a good idea, anyway." said Colette.

Ian stood in the doorway to the room. "I'm sorry, Abby," he said.

"Did he tell you that he was going sailing just because he was mad at me?" Abby asked.

Ian shook his head.

"I wish you hadn't let him go," said Abby.

"What was I supposed to do, tie him up?"

Abby shrugged. "I'm gonna go home, I guess. When's the next train? What a farce!"

"There's one at noon," said Ian.

"I'm gonna go with her," said Colette. "Abby, we'll both go."

"Look, Abby is not a wounded animal," said Ian. "I'm sorry Abernathy went off, but it's not my fault."

Colette was furious. How could Abernathy treat Abby like a piece of Kleenex? He brought her up here, bought her a vest, and then just left her alone in his house to get home by herself. "He's a shit," said Colette.

"Hey, wait a minute," said Ian. "He's my friend."

"Some friend. How come he's such a great friend, huh? How can you hang around him?"

"You've got no right talking about him like that," said Ian.

"He's a snob. He calls Abby a JAP, and now he just goes off. He's some friend to have."

"Look, Colette. You're not my mother," yelled Ian. "And you're not Abby's mother. I don't need anyone calling my friend a shit."

"Will you two please stop it?" cried Abby. "Here I'm the one who gets dumped, and you two fight."

Colette started to tell Ian she was sorry.

But Ian looked furious. "Colette would rather fight anytime. If she were in charge of the world, she'd blow it up in a minute."

"I wouldn't," cried Colette.

"You would, too."

Abby stared at them both.

"Let's go," said Colette. "Say good-bye to Abernathy for us," she said in an exaggeratedly polite voice. "Come on, Abby. Let's get out of this house. I don't want to spend another minute here. We can walk to the train station. It isn't far."

"Oh, how dramatic!" mocked Ian.

Colette and Abby walked out.

"Look, you'd better not break up with Ian because of me," said Abby as they closed the front door behind them.

"I'm not. The whole thing stinks." Colette looked back up the driveway. She half-expected Ian to come down to tell her that she hadn't gone too far, that this was just one of their "practice" fights. She thought how comforting it would be if he came out and started teasing her again. But the driveway was empty.

He was gone.

Chapter Thirteen

Colette couldn't believe that it was all over. But the phone stayed silent—for three weeks. She blamed herself. Nobody could love someone who screamed at him that his friend was a shit. But he wasn't blameless either. Colette just wished that he would call so that they could figure out what went wrong.

On the Friday before Thanksgiving vacation, Abby was spending the night at Colette's house. They had agreed to play at a party that weekend and they were supposed to be rehearsing, but the rehearsal wasn't going well. They decided to take a break.

"You're thinking about Ian, I can tell," said Abby.

Colette nodded. "I thought having a broken heart was supposed to make you sing better. Aren't I supposed to have more soul? How come I sound like a toad?"

"You don't sound like a toad. More like a tadpole. I told you, you should call him."

"I can't. Look, if he wanted to have anything to do with me, he would have called. What if he hangs up on me?"

"You could call him and hang up. Actually, I've been doing that to Abernathy. I call the dormitory and then when he gets on the phone and I hear his voice, I hang up."

"Abby, you're kidding! What if he guesses it's you?"

"I can't help myself. I know I shouldn't call him. Then this urge comes over me, and I reach for the phone."

Colette put down her guitar. "You really do call the dormitory?"

"I've done it a dozen times," said Abby. "But half the time he hasn't been there. It's like my fingers have a mind of their own. You know, 'let your fingers do the walking.' I'm sitting and doing my homework and the next thing I know, I'm dialing the number. The shit is going to hit the fan when my father gets the phone bill. Those are all long-distance calls."

"Abby, you're nuts. If I did that, I'd be scared stiff that Ian would know it's me, right through the wires." Colette stared at the phone as she spoke, wishing it would ring. She remembered lying in the bed with Ian's arms around her—how he would sometimes tease her when she least expected to be teased. She remembered the way his face looked when she would get mad for no reason. "I miss him," she said.

"I know," said Abby. "I liked the two of you together. Ian was so comfortable to be with. I wish I could fall for someone like him. Except, my fate is to fall for someone who dumps me to go sailing. I mean, it's so tacky."

"Ian dumped me, too."

"He didn't exactly, you know. You gave

him a hard time. I think he thought you *wanted* to break up with him."

Colette stared at Abby. "Do you think so?"

Abby nodded her head. "I never understood why you two had such bad fights."

"We came from two such different worlds," said Colette.

Abby hooted. "Spare me. What a cliché! Which two different worlds?"

"He was so Waspy, so upper-class."

Abby shook her head. "I've already told you—I think you're *totally* nuts. It never made such a difference to you before. I think you were just scared because he was *so* nice. You were looking for something to give him a hard time about, and so you picked on him for being a Wasp."

"I didn't pick on him."

"You did, Colette. You were much harder on him than you'd ever be on me."

Colette bit her lip. "How come what you say makes me nervous?" she asked.

"Because it's the truth. I don't think his being a Wasp scared you half as much as his being nice."

"But wasn't he a snob?"

Abby shook her head. "You say you come from two different worlds. Well, I think that's a crock. Clarion is a privileged school, too, you know. But even if you're right, why does that mean you can't get along? Who says people are supposed to stay only with people who are exactly like them? What a boring, cloned world."

"Now you make it sound like it was all my fault."

Abby grinned at her. "If the shoe fits . . ."

"You think *I* was to blame for our breaking up."

"Colette, I know this comes as a shock to you. We're best friends, and I love you, but you're not perfect."

Colette started to laugh. "I'm not?"

Abby shook her head. "Hardly . . . and you were a lot less than perfect with Ian."

"So you think I should call him and apologize."

"It wouldn't hurt."

Colette stared at the phone. "I could just call and not say anything, couldn't I? I mean, I could just hear his voice, then I'd hang up." Colette shook her head. "This is stupid. They're both out of our lives. Even if I wasn't fair to Ian, he doesn't want me anymore. Forget them. Let's do that new song over."

They started to practice, but it was clear that neither of them had their hearts in it. The phone rang and Colette went to get it. The phone never rang without a jolt flashing through her. She felt a quickening of every nerve as she wondered if it was Ian. Maybe he had ESP and knew that she wanted to talk to him.

Colette picked up the phone. "Colette?" The voice sounded familiar, but Colette couldn't place it.

"It's Abernathy . . . Jim Abernathy."

Colette sucked in her breath. "Hi . . ." She could hear that she sounded out of breath.

"How have you been?" Abernathy asked.

"Fine, just fine." Colette wondered if they were going to have an exchange of polite chitchat, as if this were a normal conversation, as if the last time she had seen him had been a perfectly conventional weekend.

"That's good . . . that's good."

"How are you doing?" Colette asked, feeling like an idiot for being so polite. Why didn't she have the nerve to ask him why in the hell he was calling her? She wondered whether Ian had put him up to it.

"I'm doing just fine, looking forward to Thanksgiving vacation. I can use the break."

"Can't we all?"

Abby had come to the telephone stand and was looking at her quizzically. Colette waved her away.

"So what are you doing for Thanksgiving?" Abernathy asked.

Colette stared at the phone. It was like she was talking to some distant uncle who barely knew her. Why was he interested in what she was doing for Thanksgiving, for God's sake?

"Well, we have a turkey and all that. Abby's family and my family and my uncle and his family usually get together."

Colette thought that by at least mentioning Abby she might get Abernathy to say something that didn't sound as if he were reading from a script.

"Sounds nice . . . very nice. We always have a very stuffy dinner."

"Well, if it has to be stuffy, Thanksgiving is the day for it—get it?—stuffy, stuffing . . ."

Colette saw Abby groan to herself and put her hand over her eyes. Colette poked her with her elbow.

"Look, Abernathy," said Colette. Abby did a double take at the sound of Abernathy's name. She stared at Colette in shock. "I hate to be rude," said Colette, "but the last time I saw you I didn't see you, if you know what I mean."

"Run that by me again."

"You know what I'm talking about. You were the disappearing host, and I'm not talking religion. Although I know you're not Catholic, you're pure Wasp, so it shouldn't bother you. I'm sorry, that just slipped out." Colette felt her cheeks turn red.

Abby had gone rigid with attention.

Suddenly Colette was furious. How dare Abernathy just call out of the blue? He had deserted Abby in the middle of a date. If he were in front of her she would punch him in the stomach as hard as she could.

Abernathy cleared his throat. "I always liked your spirit, Colette," he said.

"Yeah, I'm sure. So did your friend."

"Ian? He was a fool to let you go."

"Why don't you just go back on your precious sailboat and sail away?" Colette started to hang up on him.

Abby shook her head furiously. She tried to grab for the phone, but Colette wrestled it away. She hung up. She and Abby stood there in silence for a moment.

Abby was near tears. "He called *you!* Why did you hang up on him? Why?"

"*Abby, he's a creep.* He was just playing a little stupid game. I bet Ian was listening in on another phone. They thought they were so cool."

"Maybe he was calling 'cause he wanted to pump you about how I was. What made you talk like that? How could you make a really gross joke like that about 'disappearing host'? That was really in bad taste. You might have ruined things for me."

Colette was stunned. "But I was defending you. Abby, the guy treated you awfully."

"Abernathy is a complicated person. He's been brought up by servants. He never sees his parents, really. He doesn't know how to love."

"Great. And you were going to teach him."

"I have a lot of love to give," said Abby.

"I know, but why give it to a snob?"

"You should have just minded your own business. Ian was right. You act like my mother. Ian's mother. Abernathy's mother. Everybody's mother. And you've got it in for both Abernathy and Ian just because they're Wasps. Who cares? Now Abernathy might never call back."

Colette felt tears in her eyes. "I don't mean to act like a mother. I don't know how this happened. I just get scared that bad things will happen to you, and then I say stupid things. But he sounded creepy on the phone. I'm sorry." Colette wiped her eyes. Her nose was running.

"Colette, don't cry."

Colette sank down on the floor. "This is

awful. We never used to fight. Abby, I can't stand it."

Abby looked at her. "Come on, Col, we can fight and still love each other."

Colette looked up at her. "We can?" She sniffed.

Abby nodded. "I bet all best friends fight all the time. Probably if we didn't fight, we'd drift apart."

"We never fought before," Colette said. "Maybe we should consider giving up boys altogether. We don't seem very good at it. You've got to admit our first serious try was a disaster."

"I still argue that Ian wasn't so bad."

"Yeah, and Abernathy is a poor misunderstood rich boy?"

"Well, I go off the deep end there, I admit, but I think Ian was different. But look, I'm not your mother, either. I can't tell you to be nice to Ian."

"It doesn't matter. Even if I wanted to be nice to him, he's gone anyhow." Colette gave Abby a worried look. "Have we made up yet?" she asked.

Abby smiled at her. "I think so. How come we can make up so easily and we can't with guys?"

"Because they are creeps," shouted Colette.

"You're right. Maybe we should write a song called 'Boys Are Creeps'. It would be a best-seller."

"Not a bad idea," said Colette. "We could dedicate it to the boys of Andover, Massachusetts."

The phone rang again. Colette and Abby both stared at it. "Do you think it's them again?" Colette asked. She was sure that Ian and Abernathy were both responsible for Abernathy's phone call.

"Do you want me to answer it?" Abby asked.

"No." Colette picked it up.

"Don't hang up, please," said Abernathy. Colette let her breath out. She hadn't realized how sure she was that it would be Ian who called back. Hearing Abernathy's voice was a disappointment.

"What do you want?"

"I didn't call to have a fight," said Abernathy.

"Look, Abby is here and we're trying to rehearse. We're playing at a party this Friday night, and . . ." Colette wanted Abernathy to know that in no way would she ever consider going out with him and hurting Abby. She hoped her tone would let him know.

To her surprise, Abernathy acted thrilled that Abby was there, as if Abby were a friend of his he hadn't seen in a while but wanted to be in touch with. "Oh, great, Abby is there, and you two are still playing together. And if you're playing Friday night, maybe you're free Saturday. That's wonderful."

"Wonderful?"

"Yeah, well, see, that's sort of why I called. I'm having a party in Boston on the Saturday night of Thanksgiving weekend, and I was thinking it would be terrific to have the two of you play."

"Are you nuts?"

Abernathy chuckled as if Colette were being just adorable to ask such a question.

"No. Come on—no hard feelings. And I'd pay you. It would be a gas."

"You are nuts."

Abernathy chuckled indulgently again. "You talk it over with Abby and call me back, okay? And tell her I send my love. Tell her also that if she wouldn't hang up so fast when she calls, I'd tell her myself. 'Bye now." Abernathy hung up.

"That guy is bananas," said Colette. "He's a pure banana through and through." Colette began pacing up and down and around the room. "He and Ian—I'm sure they cooked it up together. Can you believe it?"

"Stop pacing and tell me what he said."

"They, or he—I'm sure Ian was listening in—they thought it would be cute if you and I played at a party Abernathy is giving the Saturday night of Thanksgiving weekend. Of all the nerve! He also said to send you his love. I tell you, he's a banana."

"Colette, will you slow down and tell me what he said?"

Colette couldn't slow down or even sit down. "Oh, by the way, he does know it's you who's been calling. He said, 'Send Abby my love, and by the way, tell her that if she wouldn't hang up, I'd tell her myself.' I tell you, they're both psychotic."

"He said, 'Send Abby my love'? Those were

his words?" Abby had grabbed Colette's arm and forced her to sit down. "Send Abby my love?"

"Abby, he was just being cute. He's terrible."

Abby giggled. "So he knew it was me, and I could see him again if we sing at his party."

"You are not seriously considering saying that we'll play at his stupid party."

Abby looked thoughtful. "You know, you use the word *stupid* too much. No offense, but lately it's almost the only word out of your mouth."

"Now, *you* sound like *my* mother. Stop changing the subject! I wouldn't go play at his party for all the money in the world. Do you hear me?"

"I thought we were a team. That we made decisions together. This isn't a fascist state. I've got a say."

"But Abby, we can't go. What if they both have other dates? What if it's just something they've cooked up to get back at us or something?"

"Don't be paranoid. And we could cook up something ourselves."

"What?"

"Remember, we were just talking about writing a song called 'Boys Are Creeps.' What if we wrote the song . . . and we sang it at the party? We could write a terrific song. Wouldn't that be something?"

"Abb . . ." Colette paused. She was about to say, "That's stupid." Abby was right. She was using that word too much, ever since she and Ian had broken up. She didn't want to call Abby stupid again.

"Come on, Colette. It would be fine. We'd be in control. We always are when we perform. We could wear something really neat, and they'll eat their hearts out that they couldn't have us. We'll get something purple and glittery!"

Colette began to hum. "Boys are creeps . . . boys are creeps . . . they creep into your heart!" she sang softly.

"That's great!" exclaimed Abby. She sat at the piano and began thumping out a driving beat. It worked.

Colette listened to her. She liked the opening lines. The words were short and sharp, and they'd be easy to remember. She pictured Ian looking up at her while she sang, looking at her the way he had that first day at the school fair. He'd know that she was singing that song to him.

Abby kept playing around with the tune.

Colette sat down next to her at the piano. She sang.

"Boys are creeps
They creep into your heart
Boys are creeps
They creep into your heart
Boys are creeps
They tear your soul apart . . ."

"That's fantastic," said Abby. "That's our refrain. Now, the verse will keep the reggae beat."

Colette tentatively sang a possible next verse.

> "Like creeping vines
> Their touch makes you cling
> Their tongues tell lies . . .
> Their kisses tell lies . . ."

"Hold it," said Abby. "You're going too fast." She continued trying to work out the melody. "'Their touch makes you cling' is hard to sing."

"That's a rhyme."

"I know, but rhyming 'lies' twice is sort of cheating. I like the part of creeping vine. I like it! I like it!"

"I do, too!" said Colette. "This may be the best thing we've done. Let's keep going." The half-formed song kept repeating in Colette's head. She kept seeing Abby and herself performing in front of a shocked Ian and Abernathy.

Colette and Abby grinned at each other. *"Boys are creeps!"* They sang loud. They sang strong. Colette concentrated on the chords. *"Boys are creeps!"* she shouted as they ended the song.

She thought of the next line, "They creep into your heart." Ian had crept into her heart, but would she ever get him back? Colette doubted that the song would win him, but at least she would leave him something to remember her by. He'd never forget her.

Chapter Fourteen

Finally, the day of the party arrived. Colette and Abby had rehearsed more than they ever had before. They rehearsed so intensely that everyone in both their families had learned their new song.

"I think it's wonderful that she and Abby have started to write their own songs," said her mother at breakfast. "It's kind of thrilling."

"Thrilling to have to listen to 'Boys Are Creeps' ten thousand times?" asked Mr. Gordon.

"The song is cute," said her mother. "I'm sure it's meant to be taken as a joke, isn't it?"

"Right, Mom," said Colette. "It's all a joke."

Colette's mother glanced at her daughter, but she didn't contradict her.

"Well, I just don't think that Colette should let her music take over her life," complained her father.

"It hasn't. Give me a break. My marks aren't bad."

"They're not bad. But they're not wonderful. You have to do better if you want to get into one of the top schools."

"Oh, Dad. When are you going to face it that I'm not brilliant? I do well enough."

"Sweetheart, I want more for you than just

'well enough.' I know what you're capable of. Remember, you're my little girl."

"Little girls have to grow up," Colette muttered under her breath.

Her father heard her. He caught Colette's eye. "I know," he said with no trace of sarcasm in his voice. Colette realized how rarely she looked straight at her father. Their eyes held for several seconds.

"I'm sorry, Dad," Colette said.

"You have nothing to be sorry for. I mean it. I'm sorry I got on your back. I know you're talented, and you're smart, too. I'm proud of you. I guess at times I don't show it."

"I love you, Dad," said Colette.

Her father smiled at her. "I love you, too." He coughed. "What time is your party tonight?"

"It's at eight. Abby's father is going to drive us."

"I just wish I could be there when you sing your new song. I don't suppose you want any fans there?" Her mother sounded hopeful.

Colette groaned. She could just imagine what her mental state would be like if her mother showed up at the party.

"Only kidding," said her mother. Colette laughed. She realized that her parents knew that she was nervous. They were trying to help her relax. She got up from the table.

"I'm going over to Abby's, okay? We'll do a final run-through and then just hang out. I'm gonna spend the night over there after the party, okay?"

"That's the second 'okay' in one sentence,"

said her father. "You must really be nervous."

Colette forced herself to smile at her father. "No, I'm not. It's just a party."

Colette went up to her room. She packed her knapsack, putting in the purple chamois shirt Ian had bought her. It was part of the plan. Then she said good-bye to her parents and rode her bike over to Abby's.

Colette could feel the breeze coming from the northeast. It looked like rain, so she locked up her bike under the eaves of Abby's house. Dana greeted her at the door. "Boys are creeps," she said.

"You got it," said Colette. Just being out of her own house made her feel better. "Where's Abby?"

"She's in the basement. She's real hyper."

Colette laughed. Dana was only seven years old. What did she know about being hyper?

Down in the basement, Abby was playing the piano, a Ray Charles blues song. Colette listened to her. Abby really was good. They were planning on singing that song tonight. It was a great song that warned lovers to be good to each other.

Abby looked up at the end of the song. "I didn't even know you were there."

"You sounded terrific. If that doesn't make them cry in their beer, nothing will."

"Let's practice our song. Get your guitar." Abby sounded tense.

Colette plugged in the guitar and tuned up. "Dana warned me you were hyper."

"Just get ready," snapped Abby. "Yesterday we sounded lousy on this song. I want to get it right."

Colette shot Abby a dirty look. She hit a chord and started to sing. "Abby's a creep, she crept into my heart."

Abby grinned, her face visibly relaxing. She played the notes on the piano and joined in the chorus.

When they finished the song, Abby looked at her. "You know, Lennon and McCartney wrote better than we do."

"Well, they were at it longer. Anyhow, let's add a Beatles song tonight. It'll remind them of our first date. Come on, let's practice."

They worked on their repertoire on and off all day. Finally, they put their instruments away. They knew that they had to rest their voices.

Neither Colette nor Abby could eat much dinner, but that wasn't unusual before they performed. Finally, it was time to go upstairs to get dressed.

They had chosen their outfits carefully. Each had bought a lavender leotard with a lace edge around the top. The leotards looked like camisoles but fit tighter. Over the leotards they would wear the purple chamois shirts, but the shirts would be worn open.

Colette was wearing jeans, because she felt most comfortable playing in them, but Abby was wearing a miniskirt made out of black sweat-shirt material, and black tights. They both wore soft, white leather jazz shoes so that they could dance around easily when they played.

Abby rolled up the sleeves of her chamois shirt. "That looks terrific," said Colette, doing the same to her shirt. "It looks punk-preppy."

Abby licked her lips as she looked at herself in the mirror. "Doesn't this remind you of the night I met Abernathy for the first time?"

"Yeah, I was thinking the same thing. Well, tonight is our revenge. You look sensational."

"So do you. But let's not call it revenge. This is a night for love. I truly believe they invited us 'cause they both wanted to apologize."

Colette felt a tremor of fear for Abby, fear for herself. She was sure that whatever was going on in Abernathy's head, apologizing wasn't part of it.

She wanted to warn Abby, but she hesitated. Abby was so excited, so sure that something good was going to happen. Colette didn't want to be the one to ruin it for her. She remembered what Abby had said about acting like her mother. Maybe part of being a best friend was letting Abby keep her hopes up.

"What's the matter?" asked Abby. "Are you nervous about seeing Ian?"

"He might not even be there. I'm sure he went to New York to see his parents."

"I'll bet you he's there, and I bet you get back together tonight."

"That's crazy."

"Then bet me."

"Well, maybe he'll be there, but no way are we gonna get back together. You'd lose."

"It's a bet."

"What are we betting?"

Abby thought. "Why don't you bet me that I'll get back with Abernathy? That way it will be the four of us again. We both win."

We both lose, Colette thought to herself, but she decided she wouldn't tell Abby that. Abby needed to believe that what she had with Abernathy had been good, and Colette felt she couldn't be the one who told her that she was lying to herself.

They went downstairs to pack their equipment into the Kleins' station wagon. "You two look fabulous!" exclaimed Abby's father. "You look like a million dollars."

"I wish that's what we were getting paid," said Abby.

"Well, it's what you are worth. Seriously, you two, you both look wonderful. Really special tonight. Lucky guys."

"Daddy," said Abby in a complaining voice. Colette recognized that voice. It was just like her own when she talked to her father. "This is just a gig. We're not going on some twerpy teenage date."

"Forgive me for complimenting you," said Abby's father. "Colette, you don't mind if I tell you that you look beautiful, do you?"

Colette couldn't help smiling. "No." Abby's father had made her feel terrific. She felt much more confident. If Ian did show up,

well, she would know at least that she looked
good.

The promised storm had arrived, and it
was a true Northeaster. The rain came down
sideways, lashing at the few leaves that
remained and sending them flying from the
trees.

"Great night for a party," said Abby's father as he helped them carry the last of their
equipment into the car.

"Probably half the kids won't show up,"
grumbled Colette, thinking that even if Ian
had planned on returning to Massachusetts
early for the party, he might be stuck in New
York because of the storm. The rain ham-
mered at the windows of the car.

"Where exactly is this party? You said it
was on Beacon Hill," said Abby's father.

"I have the address," said Colette, aware
that her voice was shaking. The address
Abernathy had given them was just across
the Charles River in one of the oldest and
most prestigious sections of Boston.

"Very posh neighborhood."

"I told you that the guy goes to Andover,"
said Abby in that annoyed voice. Colette felt
sorry for both Abby and her father. She knew
that Abby couldn't help the way she was
sounding. She was just nervous, and everything her father said was wrong.

They drove the rest of the way in near
silence. Colette was surprised when they
arrived. She had expected Abernathy to live
in an old ornate brownstone. Instead, the
address turned out to be a modern apartment

building with a doorman waiting for them. The doorman was dressed in a double-breasted gold satin coat with red braid across his chest.

"He looks like he belongs in Sergeant Pepper's Band," whispered Abby.

"Here goes nothing," said Colette.

They told the doorman that they wanted the Abernathy residence. "Yes, I was told to expect a girl's band," said the doorman.

Abby and Colette looked at each other. Colette felt her heart start to race. "Make room for the Punk Preppies," whispered Abby.

"Do you girls want me to help you bring your stuff upstairs?" asked Abby's father.

"No," said Colette and Abby in unison. Mr. Klein laughed. "That sounds definite. Okay, have a good time. You girls are going to take a taxi home, right?"

"Right, Dad. Don't wait up for us. It might be late."

Abby's father groaned. "In my days, I would never have told my father not to wait up for me. It was a given that he would."

"Good night, Dad," said Abby pointedly.

"This way, ladies," said the doorman. "We can take your equipment up in the freight elevator."

"Right," whispered Colette. "We wouldn't want our amps to scratch their fancy elevators."

Abby seemed distracted. "Colette, I just had the most incredible thought. What if there's no party, and it was all just a plot to see us again? Could it be?"

"Don't sweat it," said Colette, but she had secretly had the same thought. It would be so romantic. They would walk in expecting the room to be full of preppy, snobby kids they had never met, and instead, Abernathy and Ian would be standing there with shit-eating grins on their faces. Ian would be holding a rose, like that day when he had showed up at her house after their first date, and he would tell her how much he had missed her and how sorry he was. "It was all a terrible misunderstanding," he would say.

But when the elevator stopped, Colette could hear the sounds of the party down the hall. She knew her daydream was just that—a fantasy.

Abby suddenly looked upset. Her face had crumbled, and she looked like she was going to cry. Colette had a feeling that she looked the same.

"Hold it," she said to Abby. "We are not slinking in there like a defeated army. What's our motto?"

"Boys are creeps," said Abby, but she didn't sound like she meant it.

"How do we get by?"

Abby smiled at her, a more genuine smile. "With a little help from our friends. Only let's not sing out of key."

"Okay. Let's go."

They rang the bell, but the noise was so loud from the stereo that no one answered. Colette shrugged and opened the door.

The place was filled with kids. Most of them looked a little older than Colette and Abby. The boys were dressed in slacks and sports jackets. The girls all looked over-dressed, in stockings and high heels and dresses that came to about their knees. The party seemed to be divided into two distinct groups, those brave enough to talk and those trying to look as if they *could* talk if they wanted to but had chosen not to.

"I think we're the only ones in purple," whispered Abby.

"I think we're the only ones who aren't plastic," said Colette.

Abernathy waved to them from a corner. Colette waved back. She looked around the room more closely. No, her first reaction was right. Ian was not at the party. She felt defeated.

Abernathy made his way through his friends. "Hey," he said. "I won my bet."

"What bet?" Colette asked. Abby looked as if she had been struck dumb.

"I bet that you would show."

Colette didn't want to ask him if he had made his bet with Ian.

"You girls look terrific." He looked down at Abby. "Thanks for wearing 'our' shirt."

"It's mine now," said Abby. "Or do you want it back?"

"Hey, don't bite my head off. I'm just glad you're here." He put his arm around Abby's shoulder. Abby shrugged it off. "Where do you want us to set up our equipment?" she asked coldly.

Colette was surprised by her tone of voice and proud of her. She wasn't sounding at all like a doormat. Abernathy pointed to a corner by a terrace. They were twenty-five stories up, and the lights from the Prudential building and from the Government Center shone beautifully, making Boston look almost like New York City.

Abernathy helped them carry their equipment to the corner. As they were setting up, Colette glanced out on the terrace. Even though the rain was still pouring down, a couple was out there, standing close to each other. They were protected by the overhang from the terrace above them, and they had a smug look about them, like two people who really cared about each other at a party where everyone else was anxious. The girl had her arm around the boy's waist, as if she were pretending to be afraid of heights. The guy was pointing to something down below. He turned back to say something to the girl, and Colette caught his face in the light. It was Ian. She felt as if she wanted to die.

Chapter Fifteen

Colette glanced up at the audience. She and Abby were near the end of their set. Ian was watching her. She looked back down at her guitar and hit the wrong note. The amp gave off a high-pitched squeak. "Shit," mumbled Colette.

Abby shot her a worried look.

The music was going terribly. Colette decided that it was a myth that the show must go on. This was one night that they should have packed it in. Their voices sounded metallic and off pitch. The kids at the party had talked loudly through the set, making Colette feel like the music was intruding on their good time.

They were nearing the end of the set. Abby shifted from the bass to the piano. She played the thumping chords of their new song. It was their finale.

Colette gritted her teeth as she picked up the melody on her guitar, pushing the rhythm into the reggae beat it needed. *What the hell,* she thought to herself. *At least I have Abby*.

"Boys are creeps!" Colette sang out.

"They creep into your heart!" sang Abby.

For the first time in the evening, the kids at the party stopped talking and started listening. Colette saw several girls start to smile self-consciously.

The reggae beat kept the words playful. Colette threw herself into the song. Abby caught her mood. The two of them played with the melody and the rhythm. They exchanged glances. They knew that for the first time in the evening they were finally playing.

"Their tongues tell lies
Their fingers tell lies
Their kisses lie in wait
They're gone and then you hate."

When they sang the chorus, some of the kids joined in with the bouncy beat.

"Boys are creeps
They creep into your heart."

Abby and Colette grinned at each other. Colette hit the last note and swung the neck of her guitar out at the audience like a machine gun. She purposely didn't point it at Ian.

Abernathy led the applause, holding his hands high. He nodded knowingly at Abby. Abby stood up at the piano and made a slightly mocking curtsy to him. Colette licked her lips, acknowledging the applause.

"More! More!" Abernathy led the cry for an encore.

Abby whispered in Colette's ear. "Change

of pace. The Ray Charles song 'You Always
Miss the Water when the Well Runs Dry.'"

Colette pushed her hair back with her
hand. She knew why Abby wanted to sing
that song. She wanted Abernathy to listen
and mourn for what he had lost. Well, what
else were the blues for?

Abby sat back down at the piano. She
played the opening bars nice and slow. Colette kept the guitar soft. They played the
melody through once without singing, to give
the audience a chance to get used to a slow
blues beat and to bring the excitement down.

Then Abby sang the first verse in her low
alto.

Colette came in on the refrain, moving
close to the microphone, harmonizing with
Abby, reaching and finding the high notes.

Colette took the next verse, feeling the
words as she sang. She was nervous, but she
kept her voice slow. She stretched out the
words.

Together she and Abby took the last verse.
They hit the last note in perfect harmony.

Abby got up from the piano and hugged
her. "We were sensational!" Abby whispered.

Colette hugged her back.

They bowed again and put down their
instruments. Abernathy came up and told
them they were wonderful. Abby looked
flushed. Abernathy kept his arm around
Abby, as if she were his prized possession.

Colette felt lost. "You were just wonderful,"
a boy gushed. He was nice-looking in a bland

way. He reminded Colette of the first time she met Ian, but this boy wasn't Ian. Colette thanked him and started to pack up her guitar. She felt a desperate need to leave the party.

"Colette, can I talk to you?" Ian held a beer can stiffly. His arm was rigid. His jaw seemed locked tight.

"Hi," said Colette shyly. "I was just going to take off."

"Please, I've got to talk to you. Get your coat and come out on the terrace."

"I saw you out there before. Is she your date?"

"She wasn't a date. She's just somebody I know. I knew you were coming, and I was scared to see you, so I got her to go on the terrace with me. I couldn't stand the suspense of waiting for you."

Colette lowered her eyes. From the very first time they'd met, Ian had surprised her by the things that he said, the way he blurted out what he was feeling. She had known from the start that she could trust his words to reflect his thoughts. She knew that wasn't true of all boys. She stopped herself. She was being unfair again. It wasn't even true of her. She rarely told Ian what she was really feeling.

"I missed you," she found the nerve to say. "I wanted to apologize for some of the things I said. I was mad at Abernathy, but it wasn't your fault."

Ian sighed. "I can't believe you're saying that. I thought you hated me."

"I wanted to call you and tell you I was sorry, but I didn't have the nerve," admitted Colette.

"And I didn't have the nerve to call you. I was afraid."

Colette smiled at him. "I guess that makes us both cowards. At least we have that in common."

Ian stared at her.

"That's a joke," said Colette quickly. "I don't really think you're a coward. You were the one who always had the nerve to say what was on your mind." She paused.

"You weren't too bad in that department yourself. You made me think. I realized that half the reason I hang around Abernathy is that I want to be like him, you know, good-looking, cool."

"I like you much better the way you are. I just didn't show it to you. I felt bad about that."

"Oh, Jesus, Colette, I love being with you. I didn't want to mess it up."

Once again his words surprised her.

"It's me who messes up all the time," said Colette. "I just seem to go crazy. We seemed to be getting along fine, and then suddenly it's like you can't do anything right and I hate you."

"I noticed. When you got so mad at me up in Manchester and it wasn't my fault, I thought, this is just too crazy for me. But I missed you so much. I just like being with you so much."

"But how can you like being with me

when I get mad at you all the time?" asked Colette.

"I don't like those times. I like the other times."

"It's crazy," said Colette. "Sometimes, maybe Abby will annoy me a little bit, but I never screech at her the way I do at you. Abby thinks that I'm unfair to you."

"Maybe friends are different from lovers. Nothing Abernathy does gets to me the way you can."

"Well, that's a good thing," said Colette with a laugh.

"I guess we just have different standards for friends than for somebody we're involved with," said Ian.

"Double standard," said Colette. "That's what Abby said I had. She thinks I was mean to you."

Ian wrinkled his nose. "You were terribly mean to me. I think it will take you a long time to make it all up to me. Come on, let's go outside."

Somebody had turned the stereo on, and it was hard to talk. Colette looked around the party. Abby was drinking beer and laughing with Abernathy and a group of his friends. Instantly Colette felt angry all over again. "I don't think I should leave Abby."

"You want to tie her up," said Ian.

"What are you talking about?"

"Well, you're worried that Abernathy will hurt her again, aren't you?"

"He will, you know."

"I know. He probably will. But he sort of

likes Abby, too. She can take care of herself. She won't die if Abernathy makes a play for her again."

"But she shouldn't just let him think she's so easy. I know Abby. She'll get in trouble."

"She'll survive."

Colette looked over at Abby again. Abby saw her and smiled a big smile. She looked happy and bouncy. Colette knew that Ian was right. Half of Abby might get very romantic about Abernathy and about how good-looking he was, but a healthy part of her would always laugh at herself. Abby's sense of humor would always save her. It was her own lack of humor where Ian was concerned that worried Colette.

"Are you sure you don't want to be with that other girl?" Colette asked. "She was very pretty."

Ian groaned. "What have we been talking about? Come on." He half-shoved her out the door onto the terrace. The rain had stopped, but the air was cold.

Ian put his arms around her.

"Wait a minute," said Colette. "We can't just make up like this. We haven't figured anything out."

Ian kissed her.

Colette rubbed his back. She looked up at him. "On the other hand," she said. "Maybe figuring everything out has been overrated."

They kissed again.

ELIZABETH LEVY has written more than twenty-five books, among them *Come Out Smiling*; *The Computer that Said Steal Me*; *Struggle and Lose, Struggle and Win*; as well as the *Jody and Jake* mystery series. Her books for younger readers include *Lizzie Lies a Lot*; *The Shadow Nose* and the popular *Something Queer* series. Ms. Levy grew up in Buffalo, New York and currently lives in New York City.